Whispering Winds of Appalachia

WHISPERING WINDS OF APPALACHIA

John Ellington

Paperback: 979-8-9895088-0-8
Ebook: 979-8-9895088-1-5

Whispering Winds of Appalachia is a work of fiction. The names, characters, businesses, places, events, locales, and incidents are either products of my imagination or used in a fictitious manner. Any resemblance to actual persons, living or dead, or actual events are coincidental.

To my best friend, Chris,

Thank you for always helping me believe that the next great adventure is just around the corner...

To Cameron,

Thank you for always being my biggest supporter and for listening to every rendition of this story. I never could have finished it without you.

Chapter One

JUNE 18, 2018

AS THE MORNING rays reveal the rich, green Appalachian mountainside, feathered layers of mist crawl out of the valleys and reach for the heavens. I've always imagined them to be wayward spirits, at last surrendered from the mountain waterways. Upon their ascent, the warmth of dawn thins and consumes what's left of the fleeting wisps. I guess that's why I never left. There is a quiet peace and a feeling of safety in the mountains. At moments when I felt the pull of the outside world, I could never find the strength to crawl out of the valleys myself. I am home in these hills. I belong to the rivers. Besides, I'm getting old.

This morning is like hundreds of mornings I've descended this path. The trail looks just as it did when I first happened upon this valley; even the shortcuts are intact. The still thickness of the summer air welcomes me with the sweetness of cedar, the richness of trodden earth, and the fullness of the alive forest, each plant and animal contributing to the appreciable mosaic. The awakening calls of robin, tanager, and thrush permeate through the dense canopy and overlay the gentle but eternal bubbling of the small creek that runs with the trail. Rhododendron is now in full bloom. The waxy green tunnel through which the water flows is dotted with soft pink flowers.

As I make my way down into the valley, I pass my favorite tree, an eastern white pine that sits on the right edge of the trail, casting its shadow on decades of souls that have passed under its arms. As always, I stop and study its details, watching and waiting as if I expect it to say something. I place my hand on its weathered, aging bark, feeling the textured topography of the moist, dew-ridden outer wood, the tree's skin. Looking past it, I see a familiar sight. A small stand of demoralized hemlocks sulk at the edge of the woods, defeated by the adelgid. In a way, they remind me of myself, with their old, heavy limbs and dying leaves. I suppose that's one thing that *has* changed over the years—me and the hemlocks.

I continue until I reach a fork in the trail and a small bridge. Crouching with one knee pressed to the old wooden planks, I stretch my neck and peer over the edge and observe the water beneath. This time of year, the water is mostly clear, with the occasional pink petal floating lazily by, on its way to the bigger rivers. The clouds have not wet the forests in over a week, and the small stream is only flowing at half strength. Nonetheless, I spot what I am looking for—what I have always looked for.

As soon as my body is raised high enough to give my eyes a clear path to the water, a small, almost translucent shadow darts quickly from the riffle to the undercut bank of the stream. The Appalachian brook trout. I know with the water low and crystal clear, I will spook any fish near the bridge. In all my years of traversing the footbridge, only once have I ever caught anything from this spot, in the autumn when the water turns tea-colored from the tannin of decaying fall leaves.

In the beginning of my love affair with fly fishing, when I was fifteen years old, I would never pass up a trout that I could see. My youthful and naïve mind thought catching was the purpose of fishing. Adrenaline would course through my veins and affect its warm energy every time I saw trout, especially a brook trout. Since then, I have learned to find a content peace just seeing them exist in their wild, remote streams high in the ridges of blue. Nowadays, more times than not, I don't even bring a rod.

I feel the gaze of people I pass and try to imagine their thoughts. Do they wonder what brings an aging man alone on such a trail? Do they pity me? I do not want or need their pity, though with all I've been through, I would pity me. Occasionally, young men walk by with the longing and eagerness I once felt here. I hope they respect me and know I was once them. Many of them will find this valley a brief, transient stop on their over-arching journey of life, leaving as soon as they came, to chase future dreams and progress. Some may never walk this path again.

In my heart, though, I know now and again I pass someone whose soul will be trapped in this valley, these mountains, the creek and its trout, just like mine. When I move on, they will carry the burden for me. They will study the pine, mourn with the hemlocks, and peer over the small wooden bridge.

My knees creak as I rise and leave the bridge behind me. After several small steps, I shake off the stiff-ness of arthritis and press on. The smaller fork of the trail descends left, parallel to the stream. I am almost there. The roar of the falls begins to echo louder with each step. If you close your eyes, the valley will tell you the waterfall is not in any one direction but in all directions. The birds cease to compete with this new sound. I round the final corner, step over the old campsite, and stand at the brim of stone marking the back edge of the pool.

The shallow tail out is wide, over one hundred feet across. It is littered with flat, smooth river stones worn down by the soft hand of time. The pool gradually

deepens and narrows as it approaches the waterfall, con-
ceding the light, lucent water for a deep, welling blue.
The sun illuminates every droplet of vapor released from
the falling water, creating a curtain of light that encompasses the face of the fall with a warm glow, giving me the
sensation that I have stumbled through the gates of heav-
en. The fall itself is twenty-five to thirty feet in height
and fifteen feet across. It is fetal in comparison to the
power of nearby Whitewater Falls or to distant western
cascades. The wonder is in the relative size of the stream
this fall occupies. Only inches deep and feet across for
much of its course, this humble creek has maintained the
waterfall for thousands of years.

Though I rest my gaze on it now, I need not to
know its every detail. I see it every time I close my eyes,
and I have for over thirty years. I am intimately familiar
with its old, wrinkled face, its rock ledges, the pathway
behind the water against the wet stones. I know the trees
that border its beginning and its end. I can trace the flow
of each section of water as it mounts the precipice and
begins its journey to the pool. Lastly, I know the two
small stone cairns draped with rhododendron blooms
only paces into the woods at the top of the falls; I stacked
them.

Tall morning shadows still rest on the easternmost
bank, shrinking from west to east with each passing

minute. I slowly step out into the water and feel the coolness penetrate my boots and socks. I never wear waders in the summer, but my age has started to bolster the bite of cold. Waders have never been easy to don, though, and my joints celebrate my refusal to wear them between May and October.

I stand knee-deep now and watch the surface of the sunlit sections of the pool. *Splash!* I tie on a black-and-white "Bivisible," a fly made of feathers from the cape of a rooster. It is tied to look like an insect, though no particular species. Its size and contrasting colors function to draw the eye of eager, wild brook trout, and I have found it is one of the only flies I can still see when casting. Maybe the trout also pity me and strike out of sympathy.

I let line off the reel and begin to cast, the familiar sharp *whiss* entering the morning score. I allow the fly to gracefully drop to the water, spinning slightly after it meets the surface. Though not as close to the feeding trout as I would like, I know it will still work. I am not long idle, as the fish hits the fly almost immediately after landing. The small trout concedes quickly and allows me to pull it to the net. With wet hands, I free it from my hook and hold it with a gentle grip, its left side facing me with all its brilliance. The dark-green substrate, pale-blue halos around red-and-orange pinpoints. The bronze underbelly, dark fins with white edges. The linear patterns breaking free from the background along its dorsum. I always imagine brook trout to be female. Their vibrant beauty, graceful delicacy, and innocent sensitivity. Or maybe it's because I think of her.

The trout's smooth, scaleless body wriggles, yearning to be returned to its home. I briefly thank it for what it means to me and thank the Lord for blessing me with the ability to still find these moments. I lower my hand into the creek and watch her disappear back into the depths of the pool.

The trout I just caught was born in this stream and will probably die here in the cool water. Her family has lived here since the glaciers receded during the last age of ice. If the valley is protected, her offspring will swim these waters for many years to come, through the misty warm mornings of summer, the cooling breezy days of autumn, the gentle blanketing of white in the winter, and the revival of life each spring.

The brook trout is the most sensitive of Appalachian trout and is the only one native to these ridges and valleys. It is perfectly adapted to this serene landscape. I feel the brook trout in my soul, as I also am resistant to change, at home in the hills, and sensitive to the outside world. I once knew two others who shared this sentiment, so much so that all three souls were one with each other and with the trout. I guess it is time.

I step out of the world beneath the water's surface and begin to climb the path by the falls. How I miss the days when my legs propelled my body up the path. Now my body is pulling my weak legs under me one step at a time. I wipe small beads of sweat from my forehead before they can sting my eyes, and I catch my breath at the top of the falling water.

No path exists to the right, but again, I know the trees. I gently part branches and step into the woods. On the ground in front of me are two small stacks of stones adorned with withering rhododendron blooms. Brook and Walker. Though they are not physically in this ground, I know their souls are here. They have not braved the morning ascent out of the mountains either. The sun is waiting to consume their mist, but they are at peace here. They wait for me. I place the freshly picked blooms upon the stones and sit, alone in the woods with my friends.

Time stands still in these moments. Years of memories flood my mind. My eyes show me faces, alive and perished. They show me the mingling of souls and the shearing of hearts. I see rivers, roads, and valleys. My heart tells me what was destined to be, while my mind reminds me of the truth. In these fleeting seconds, I long for it to have been different. To think of the world with them still by my side. It wasn't my fault, yet I could have prevented it. Tears fill my eyes and begin to flow over my lids. I look down and watch them gracefully fall to the forest floor, momentarily darkening the soil before being welcomed back into the ground. I think I am ready to do what I haven't found the courage or peace to do for the last two months.

I reach into my shoulder pack and move my fly boxes to the side. Underneath is a folded piece of paper and a small, knobby wooden slingshot. As my fingers feel the texture of the paper, a tingling chill climbs my spine, branches out at my shoulders, and trickles down my arms. This is not the first time I have touched the letter. However, something about touching it in final anticipation of reading it takes an effect on my soul. With trembling hands and wet eyes, I carefully unfold the paper and hear Walker's younger voice as I read his words. "To my best friend, Chris ..."

Chapter Two

MAY 5, 1973

My family moved across the state of North Carolina from Raleigh to Transylvania County in the spring of 1973, when my father accepted a plant manager position. His new office was a large paper mill just outside Brevard in Pisgah National Forest. Despite their frequent visits to the mountains in the years leading up to the move, my parents were blissfully unaware of the challenge it would pose to permanently relocate. Families living in the Appalachian Mountains in those days were tough, loyal to their own kind, and generally uninterested in outsiders.

The dilapidated farmhouse my parents purchased resided on just under twenty acres of wooded valley bottom and five acres of sloping mountainside. The adjacent property was a small family dairy farm, Davis Milk. The owner of the dairy, Grady Davis, was said to live alone with his son, who was about my age. During our first few months there, every attempt my parents made at introduction was unsuccessful. They had walked over to the Davises' house once a week to knock on the door. Grady, whether he heard the knock or not, never answered.

After a while, my parents realized they needed to change tactics. Instead of continuing to pester their new neighbor, my mother decided to employ classic southern hospitality. Every boy claims their mom's cornbread is the best, and I'm certain that I'm the only one who's right. She always said it's because she made it with extra love. Over the years, though, my dad and I realized that *love* meant butter, a lot of butter. To this day, whenever someone adds butter to a dish, we say it's made with extra love. The cornbread my mom left on Grady's porch on May 3 was overflowing.

I woke up two days later in dire need of an adventure. Being ten years old in a new town without a single friend is desperately lonely. I heard someone my age lived next door, but thus far we had not met, and it was beginning to seem like he didn't exist. Fortunately, our property was paradise for a young boy.

The small creek that trickled cold water down the mountain past the house emptied into a larger stream on the other side of the road. Since I knew where it ended, that morning I decided to find its beginning. Knowing nothing about mountain springs, I had no expectation of what I would find or where I would find it. The only thing I knew for sure was where to start. I quickly inhaled some buttered toast, grabbed my slingshot, and flew out the back door.

Minutes later, I was ankle deep in a trickling mountain creek. After climbing the gentle slope of our back yard, the water and I disappeared into an opening in the woods framed by poplar, basswood, and yellow buckeye. Only small patches of sunlight completed the descent from the canopy to the forest floor, leaving me in a world much darker than the one outside. My morning courage was undercut by the shady solitude, but I pressed on toward my goal.

The monotonously flowing water started to take new form the farther I climbed up the mountain. Instead of sandy bottom, my feet were now walking on piles of smooth river stones. As I studied this novel creek bottom, my eyes were drawn to subtle movements. Until now I had never appreciated the vivacity of the underwater world, especially from my previous home in the Raleigh suburbs.

Several crawfish hurried away from my clumsy footsteps. I thrust my hand into the cold, clear water in an attempt to capture one but only managed to grab a small rock. Before I tossed it back into the water, I noticed something peculiar. Small, dark insects seemed to be crawling around on its underside. As fascinating as it was at the time, I had no idea these tiny aquatic insects, the primary food source of trout, would shape my entire life's course.

I continued at this slow, intentional pace for quite some time until I could no longer see the farmhouse. The creek was broken every few steps now by small waterfalls, and thus walking turned into climbing. Nonetheless, I was determined to continue my journey.

Suddenly, I was alerted by a disturbance in the woods to my right. I caught a brief glimpse of coarse, dark hair as a large creature darted between two trees only paces from the creek. My entire sense of adventure vanished in a matter of seconds, and my hand reached for the small slingshot in my pocket. I was frozen in place for what seemed like a lifetime, waiting for any sound or sign of movement. I became acutely aware of my heart, and every beat thumped at the base of my throat.

Like many kids, I was terrified of bears. My parents had warned me about wandering into the woods alone and had used them as a deterrent for my solo adventuring. They led me to believe around every turn a towering, malicious, starved bear was waiting to eat small ten-year-old boys.

As I've learned through a lifetime spent in the woods, unless cubs are around, black bears are more afraid of people than people are afraid of them. Countless times as an adult, I have walked around the bend of a trout stream and come face to face with a bear. Every time, they explode into a fit of alarmed confusion and take off into the woods as if shot from a cannon, leaving a trail of broken limbs and crushed plants. Unfortunately for me, the animal I stumbled upon that day was no black bear, but a large feral hog.

The silence was finally broken by a grunt and a sharp squeal. The seed of terror planted in my soul by the initial movement was quickly blossoming into full-blown panic. I had never heard sounds like those before, but realized I now found myself in imminent peril. Waiting no longer, I turned my back to the threat and sprinted in the opposite direction, looking for anything that might prove to be my refuge. I heard twigs break behind me and rapid beating of hooves on the forest floor; I was being chased.

Knowing I was moments from being caught, I grabbed a low-hanging branch from a welcoming beech tree and hoisted myself off the ground. I climbed several more limbs before finally looking down at my pursuer. Scratching at the bottom of my tree was a two-hundred-pound feral boar, breathing heavily after the brief pursuit. His patchy, rough brown coat was matted and covered with debris. Each side of his mouth produced a gnarled, sharp tusk. An offensive and overwhelming musk diffused from the pig into my nose, adding to the dread. As if knowing I was at my breaking point, he looked up at me and produced a demonic, shrill scream that still gives me chills to this day.

An hour or so passed with me stuck like a raccoon, treed by the most patient hog God ever created. Seeing no way out of my predicament, I briefly considered jumping and continuing our foot race down the mountain toward the farmhouse. Though confident in my speed, I decided the pig had me beat. Back to the drawing board. I was the best shot of all my Raleigh friends with my slingshot but was increasingly concerned the boar would react differently than my father's glass Coca-Cola bottles. Again, back to the drawing board. The next idea was foolproof. I would intimidate him with shouting, lots of shouting. I threw my head back, beat on my chest, and screamed at the pig.

"Get out of here, *pig*! Go on, get! Aaaaahhhhh!" If that feral hog was intimidated, he had a funny way of showing it. He sat down, looked up at me silently, and cocked his head to the side.

"What are you looking at?" I shouted to him. "Ugh, he's not scared. He's confused," I sighed to myself. I then said the only phrase I imagined appropriate for my current state, "Damn it." I'd never cursed before, but if I was going to die by a vicious hog mauling, I figured God would forgive me. My ideas running thin, I sat down in silence and continued pondering. Wondering what God would think of my language had given me a new idea. I could pray.

"God," I said, "first of all, I'm sorry for saying a bad word. I've heard Dad say it a hundred times, though, and he's the biggest Christian I know, so I'm sure you'll forgive me. Secondly, please deliver me from this giant pig. Amen." For some reason, I started getting the feeling that wasn't a good enough prayer. I ignored my mom telling me to pay attention at church, and now I was literally going to die because of it.

Just when I thought all hope was lost, I heard footsteps rapidly approaching us through the forest. Moments later, a large rock hit the boar on its flank, causing it to pivot in alarm. A second stone came flying, seemingly from thin air, and found its mark square on the beast's skull. The dull thud of impact was followed by a final squeal. The pig had met its match and took off in a rapid, chaotic retreat through the woods.

Not knowing whether the hog or its conqueror was a bigger threat, I remained motionless and silent as a grave. What I saw next baffled me to the core. Out from behind a hemlock stepped a boy, likely my age. He had disheveled, curly brown hair and looked to be about my height. His expression was plain, unbridled confusion.

"Why are you up in that tree?" the boy asked.

Dumbfounded, I responded, "Did you see that pig? He'd have killed me!"

"Killed you?" The boy erupted in a fit of laughter. "Only if you let him! That's not even a big one."

I didn't respond immediately because giant feral boars were now running and squealing through my imagination. *Bigger than that one?* I thought. *That's the last time I'll ever leave my house.*

"Who are you?" the boy asked. "This is my daddy's land, ya know."

"Oh, I didn't know that. Um, I'm Chris. I live in the white house next to the dairy."

"The dairy? You mean our dairy. You're the city slicker that moved in? That explains why you're up in a tree," he said, now walking toward the trunk. "Climb on down now, the hog's gone, probably looking for some truffles."

"You're Walker? Walker Davis?"

"Well, who else would I be?"

"Thanks for saving me. I thought I was going to be pig feed," I said.

"You're welcome." Walker stood there awkwardly as I let go of the final limb and landed on my feet at the base of the beech. "I don't think I'm supposed to be talking to you." He looked at his feet. My sense of alarm gone, I noticed for the first time Walker's clothes. His jeans were tattered, his shoes had more holes than Swiss cheese, and his shirt was missing both sleeves. My innocent, if not naïve, mind could not understand that Walker was poor, but the dirt smeared across his face added to my growing realization that Walker looked different from any of my friends back home. He looked at me and frowned. Slowly, Walker turned and started walking back through the woods in the direction from which he so valiantly came charging to save me.

"Wait!" I shouted, causing him to pause. "You could throw those rocks a lot harder with a slingshot."

"I don't have a slingshot," he said with a soft voice.

"Well, how about I trade you a slingshot for saving my life?" I reached into my pocket and pulled out my prized wooden weapon. Something in the depths of my heart told me I needed to give it to him. I held my hand out and stretched my fingers so that the slingshot was resting in my open palm.

"Really!" He came bounding back toward me. Once in front of me again, he simply waited but did not take it from me.

"Go ahead! It's yours now."

Walker's face lit up, and for the first time I witnessed the unfiltered joy and excitement that would sustain our friendship for years and years.

"You can call me Walk. My father and my best friend Brook call me that. Only my teachers and other school kids call me Walker," he said as he searched frantically for a stone to sling. I was left to wonder—if his father and a girl named Brook call him Walk and only his teachers and other "school kids" call him Walker, what do his other friends call him? Little did I know, I had just become his only other friend.

"Do you want to come see our cows?" he asked, after slinging several stones through the trees. Without waiting for an answer, he bolted off into the dense spring forest. Starved for friends, I quickly followed behind him.

After several minutes of exhaustive pursuit, we came to a clearing in the woods that marked the edge of the Davis Milk pastures. The quiet, pristine forest gave way to bright-green, rolling hills dotted with Holstein cows.

"This is the far-off pasture," Walker explained. "These are pregnant cows that have a while before calving. Be careful, though, some of the heifers can be real assholes." My mouth dropped open as the word left his mouth. I had awkwardly muttered my first swear minutes before, but only because I thought death was in short order. Walker let it roll off his tongue like any other word.

He must have noticed my shock. "What? Your parents don't cuss? Grady cusses like a sailor. Mom never liked it much, but she died last year. If you meet him, don't look surprised. He doesn't need any more reason not to like you."

"What does your dad have against me and my family?" I asked, confused.

"You ain't from here. You're just another family from the city coming here to ruin the mountains," he explained, echoing the words he undoubtedly heard come from his father's mouth.

"Well, I'm not here to ruin anything. I'd rather be back home in Raleigh anyway. I don't have any friends here."

Walker looked at me for a long time, searching me up and down. I could tell he was pondering something. I didn't say a word but looked into the distance over the pasture. His stare was starting to make me uncomfortable, as if I was cattle at a sale.

Finally, Walker spoke up. "Tomorrow is my birthday. You should come over to my house! Brook will be there. Once you meet her, you will have two friends here."

"Will your dad let me?" I asked.

"I'll convince him. He's a pushover, and that cornbread was damned good."

Chapter Three

DECEMBER 25, 1975

"CAN YOU PASS the ham Mrs. Avery?" Mr. Palmer asked across the oak table between long sips of brandy-spiked cider.

"Here you go, honey," my mother replied, as she struggled more than she anticipated passing the heavy silver platter laden with neatly stacked slices of aromatic Christmas ham. "I'm so glad you like it," she added with a warm smile.

As a thirteen-year-old boy, I only partially understood why Brook and her father joined us for Christmas dinner that year. My parents told me that Brook's mother had moved away and that we needed to make their Christmas a little more special. The rest of the details were kept secret by my parents. I began to wonder if Brook's Christmas had been special at all, while watching her fork around her food all evening, consuming almost nothing.

I decided to offer her a smile, as my mother had to her father. She weakly pressed her lips together to attempt smiling back but looked away quickly and dried her eyes with the cloth napkin for the third time that evening. *Is her mother sick?* I wondered to myself, thinking of Walker losing his mother a few years prior. I began to wish Walker was with us, since he always knew how to make Brook smile. He was her "boyfriend," a term I was still a little confused about. It seemed they were friends, just like she was friends with me. I never saw them kiss, like my parents did, but they held hands often. But then again, I held hands with Walker sometimes as we ran around the woods. Maybe being someone's boyfriend gave you permission to hold hands with a girl. I was sure I would figure it out in time.

Regardless, Walker had told me that afternoon Grady wasn't having a great Christmas and that they needed to spend the evening at home. He mentioned something about money and the farm. Walker was always talking about the farm. He seemed so grown up compared to me, which made me admire him. Since he talked about money so frequently, I assumed he and Grady had a lot of it. It wasn't for several years that I realized sometimes the people most concerned with money actually have the least amount of it.

"Brook," my father started, "how are your classes at school going? Do you have a favorite?"

Brook looked up from her plate, which was still full of food, and made eye contact with my dad. She pulled at a strand of her soft brown hair and twirled it around her finger. "Um ..." she started in a soft voice, before looking to her father for help.

"Go ahead, Brook, tell Mr. Avery what you learned in science the other day."

"Oh, that's right," she said, as her wet brown eyes seemed to brighten and subtly dry, "Mr. Smith, the science teacher, told us about metamorphosis! He said that in the spring we are going to get tadpoles—you know, baby frogs—and help them transform into adult frogs! All in the classroom!"

"That's so neat!" my mom responded to Brook, between bites of macaroni and cheese. "Isn't it so special that God created little tadpoles and taught them how to grow legs and turn into frogs?"

"Yes! And he said that if we take really good care of them in the classroom, when the project is over, we can take one home as a pet!"

"Lovely," Mr. Palmer said, rolling his eyes. "Just what we need ... a pet."

My dad chuckled and looked at me. "Chris, maybe if you get one as a pet, you can release it into the creek behind the house."

"Well, Mom said …" Brook trailed off and looked down. "Mom said we don't have time for another pet."

"Forget what your mom said, Brook," Mr. Palmer said quickly. My mom, as if on cue, stood up and started clearing the table. "You can have as many pet frogs as you want. Get over here, sweet girl!"

Brook pushed her chair away and went to her father, who lifted her up and placed her in his lap. "Well, I only want one. What am I supposed to do with more than one frog?"

"Okay then, one it is." Brook's dad leaned down and kissed the top of his daughter's head. She smiled and hugged him around his neck, burying her head in his chest.

For some reason, I started feeling uncomfortable still sitting around the table, so I stood up and carried my plate toward the kitchen, which was down a small hallway. Right before I reached the doorway, I stopped, because I heard my parents talking in hushed voices.

"It's a damn shame. I can't imagine ever leaving a young daughter like that, and right before Christmas too!" my mom said angrily. I had never heard my mother use language like that, so I froze in my tracks.

"Well, what else would she do? She can't stay now, not after having an affair. She's her hillbilly boyfriend's problem now. Good riddance, if you ask me. She wasn't worth two shits at home anyway. I never liked her. Besides, I called it two years ago when she kept coming home late. The sad part is Brook's dad probably knew about it the whole time. He just chose not to believe it."

"It breaks my heart. That poor, poor girl. Luckily, they won't be hurting for money. Thank God he was a lawyer at least." My mom furiously scrubbed her plate, removing all signs of food and likely some of the polish with it.

"I worry about him, though. Sometimes work can keep the mind occupied during a crisis like this. Did you see how much brandy he has had tonight? He needs to be careful. Drinking isn't going to bring his wife back," my dad said gravely.

"He's slurring his words a little, but what can we do? It's not our place to say anything."

I finally gathered courage to walk into the kitchen. "Here, Mom," I said as I handed her my plate.

"Come here, Chris," she said quietly as she threw her arms around me. She hugged me firmly for what seemed like two or three minutes. I still didn't understand what they meant by an "affair," but I knew it must have upset my mother in bad way and her hug was an expression of the pain she was feeling. I hugged her back. Something about the moment made me sad too, and I started to cry.

"Sweetie!" she said when she felt me sobbing. "It's going to be okay. You are going to have to be strong for Brook. She is going to be very sad, but she and her father will be okay. She's going to need you to be a good friend. Do you understand?"

I sniffled as I regained my composure. "I understand."

"You are such a good son, Chris. Your father and I love you more than you could ever know."

I tried to smile.

"So, how are things going at the plant, Bob?" Mr. Palmer asked my dad when we sat back down at the table.

"Things are actually going really well! We have increased production quite a bit since I have been here," my dad replied.

"Oh, he's being modest." My mother smiled and poked my dad below his rib cage. "*He* has increased production since he took the manager position. He just got a very big raise!"

"Congratulations," Mr. Palmer said with a joyful expression. "That's great news. That place has needed a kick in the rump for many years, if you ask me. Sounds like they've found their guy."

"It hasn't been easy. It seems like most people up here move a little slower than they did back in Raleigh."

"And a lot slower than Charleston," Mr. Palmer said, rolling his eyes. "You have to understand, mountain folk kind of live and work at their own pace. They aren't lazy by any means, but life just tends to move a little slower."

"Well, regardless of how slow life moves for them, the plant needs to keep up with demand. They can move slowly back at home every evening."

"Well," my mom interrupted, "why don't we go sit in the living room and listen to some Christmas music on the radio by the fireplace. Brook, would you and Chris like a little hot chocolate?"

"Yes please, Mrs. Avery!"

Brook and her father sat with us in the living room for several hours as we happily digested Christmas dinner. Before long, the new bottle of brandy my parents put out was empty, most of it consumed by Brook's father, who began dozing off on the couch. As I listened to the sound of popping firewood mixed with "Christmas for Cowboys" by John Denver coming from the crackly old radio, I pondered my mother's conversation with me in the kitchen.

I am going to have to be strong for Brook.

27

Chapter Four

MAY 6, 1983

FORTUNATELY FOR ME, the ground at the base of our front steps wasn't paved until the nineties. As I came flying out of the old white farmhouse that morning, thinking about fishing, my left foot caught the edge of a warped pine board on the porch, and I transformed from a land-dwelling creature into something resembling a turkey in flight. With arms erratically cutting the crisp morning air, I braced for impact at the bottom of the four-step porch. With a dull thud, my left shoulder impacted the gravel-and-clay driveway, followed by the remainder of my body. I blinked heavily and shook my head, trying to awaken my groggy mind, as I brushed a layer of dirt off my pants.

Only a minor inconvenience; I rose and hurried down the dirt path toward the cornfield, my mother hollering after me, "Chris, honey, are you all right?" This morning I would let her assume no news is good news. A clear mountain stream was calling my name, and my soul felt dried out and hollow, withdrawals from the last few weeks spent away from trout fishing. I knew I was not the only one feeling those effects.

After about a hundred paces on the road, I turned left and disappeared into the cornfield, taking a shortcut to the dairy blazed by years of friendship. Of course, the shortcut was more convenience than necessity this morning; the corn had only recently gone in the ground, and running through the middle of the field was entirely possible. As I neared the other side, the familiar rhythmic sound of the mechanical pumps met my ears. I continued running toward the source of the sound, the parlor. Approaching, I could see Grady's lean figure standing behind a group of Jerseys, partly begging, mostly cursing them toward the back of the room.

"Damn you stubborn, block-footed, good-for-nothing heifers! Get up! Get up! *Get up!*"

"Always a gentleman! Is that how you talk to your lady friends around town?" I shouted over the sound of the pumps and bellowing cattle.

"If these girls spook at you running up here like a smartass prick, Chris, it will be the end of you. Walker is in the parlor ... unless maybe you showed up to give me hand?"

"Uh, no sir"

"Then get the hell away from these Jerseys!"

I learned most of the English language in school, like the rest of the kids in town. The select words they did not teach us, however, I learned from Grady. Years of running a dairy had refined his use of expletives and curses like no man I ever knew. Don't get me wrong, he loved his cows, but you would never guess it listening to the way his tongue twisted and turned, pleading them to move. His foul mouth was not the only result of his years collecting milk.

Grady's skin layered his bones like old leather, cracked and brown with less vitality than bark. His hair was a long and mottled graying brown and always clung to his scalp in a mat of dirt and grease. If he bathed at all, the effects were quickly lost to the toil of his living. His eyes were old and tired, only partly opened to protect his aging retinas from the sun. For all his rough edges and foul language, Grady was a kind man. He had suffered through more than most, but his life left him no time for indignation. I had never known him to drink or fight, and he had always loved and supported his son, whom I was now en route to see.

I walked quietly into the herringbone parlor from the rear, the pumps drowning out all sounds and most thoughts. The mixed aroma of fresh raw milk, Holstein manure, and chemical disinfectant permeating the air grounded me in the present moment and pressed on me the feeling I was home. I had, after all, spent many early mornings and late afternoons toiling in this parlor. Standing behind one of the cows with a four-claw cluster pump in his hand was my best friend, twenty-one years old to the day.

As a young adult, Walker had chocolate-brown wavy hair that curled up around the sides and back of his hat, laden with sweat. His thin frame supported around 180 pounds of lean muscle. The daily operations around the dairy molded his body into useful machinery used to accomplish the required tasks but did not bestow the bulk of meat seen on the arms of a bodybuilder. His eyes, hazelnut with specks of green, perpetually filled with hope and the shine of optimism, now studied the quarters of the Holstein with which he was working. His lips pressed tightly together in an exhausted but dutiful grimace.

It was seven now, but I knew Walker had been milking cows since four. I could see the morning had taken its toll. The white undershirt he wore was soaked through with the wetness of labor and painted with manure to give the impression of brown tie-dye. His loosely fitting jeans were similarly sweated through and covered with white dots, the result of bleach from years of cleaning. He had not seen me yet.

Pointing at his shirt, I shouted, "Did you not tell the cows it was your birthday?"

Never startled, Walker without looking presented me with his middle finger. "If I had, they'd have probably shit on me more." Before turning his head, I saw the corner of his mouth start to rise, giving birth to crow's feet, evidence of his favorite emotion. "If your gift was helping me milk, you're about three hours late."

"Sorry, man, but my time of morning milkings has passed. You're lucky I still help some in the afternoon. Finish up with this last group and come with me. I got something for you."

No more than an hour later, Walker and I were climbing into my burnt-orange 1974 Ford Bronco, a gift from my parents when I got accepted to Brevard College three years prior. It was the envy of our friends, though I never talked much of it around Walker. It was never in the cards for Walker to attend college. Since birth, it was always expected that he would inherit and run Davis Milk, a proposition with which he had no qualms. He had never enjoyed school anyway and had a heart for manual labor. He knew the money would be short and he would be forever bound to the land. He understood he would milk cows twice a day until the second coming of Christ, but that didn't bother him. Still, I never spoke of money with Walker. There was no need. He had what he had, and I had what I had. We were content with that.

Grady harbored guilt for Walker's predestination to live the same hard life he had lived. Because of that, every summer when Brook and I weren't in school, Grady would require less of Walker and encourage him to spend the days with us. We drove down the dirt road and turned onto the curved mountain highway, leaving a lingering cloud of dust in our wake.

"Happy birthday, Walker." I reached with one arm behind his seat and pulled out a glass fifth of Jack Daniels, placing it on his lap. "This is only part of your gift. The rest is our plan for the day."

He popped the cork and took a long pull, the sweet scent of whiskey exploring the air in the cab. "If it doesn't involve a small trail, cold water, and brook trout, you can go ahead and drop me off here to finish this bottle."

"Lucky for you, Clyde told me about a new spot. It's just outside of Highlands. It sits at close to four thousand feet, has almost no foot traffic, involves a brutal hike, and allegedly is brimming over with brook trout." No one knew where Clyde came from or how long he had been here. It was speculated that he was birthed from a tree several thousand years ago. He ran a small fly shop in town that had been open since long before Walker and I were born.

Clyde usually didn't give out his own fishing spots, but he was fond of Walker. In high school, Walker would spend many a day sitting at Clyde's counter, talking about the mysteries of the world. That is, until the phone would ring and an angry voice request that Walker be sent back to school. No one else talked to Clyde the way Walker did. Most people, including myself, would pretend to listen to Clyde while picking out flies or buying other tackle, not well hiding our disinterest. We were not there to discuss politics, questions of religion, or biological phenomena. Neither were we there to discuss Clyde's past. Walker, though, was. He rarely bought anything, but just came to talk and had for years. Thus, the day before, when I had told Clyde today was Walker's twenty-first birthday, he told me about Lonesome Valley.

We passed through downtown Brevard around eight that morning and witnessed parts of the sleepy mountain town waking up. The corner coffee shop had its doors open and a *welcome* sign hanging in the window. I could almost smell the aroma of roasted beans and fresh morning pastries as we passed the wooden entryway. The local bakery had a small line of people standing by the curb. The baker had been working for several hours but had yet to invite in his patrons, who patiently awaited his fresh bread.

Walker broke the silence of the peaceful drive through town, "There goes Brook and Maddy. I can't imagine she'd be happy with me drinking at eight in the morning." The girls had just rounded the corner of one of the side streets, making their way toward the coffee shop. They were conversing and didn't notice the Bronco. Walker's head turned as we passed them, admiring his girlfriend and her best friend.

"I can drop you off if you'd rather spend the day sipping coffee and reading ..."

"Hell no," he said, laughing. "I spent all of yesterday with her, but another kind of brook is calling me today." He paused. "Chris, do you remember the jewelry my mom left me?"

"Maybe, why?"

"Well, I was able to sell it in town for a good chunk of cash."

I was shocked at this revelation, knowing where it would likely lead. I let the silence linger as he built up the courage to say what was on his mind. After all, both Brook and I had been waiting on this for years.

He stuttered forward, trying not to trip on his words like I had on the stairs just hours before, "I th-think I am going to start looking for a ring." His lips formed a sheepish smile as he tried to hold back all the emotions his words set upon his heart. Then, as if to escape the pressure, he threw the bottle back again. Thinking back on that moment, I believe he was overcome with joy but also encumbered with the weight of embarrassment. For years, the only thing in Transylvania County surer than the death and taxes was Walker and Brook. They were kindred spirits joined at the hip, seemingly since the dawn of time.

They were true junior high sweethearts. The years had ebbed and flowed as their relationship blossomed, decayed, sputtered, roared, climbed, fell, grew, and shrank, among all the other verbs in the English language. They loved each other and hated each other at times. They cried at the loss of both of their moms, albeit to different circumstances. They laughed at their fathers' unique shames, though keeping them sacred and hidden from others. Several times they threatened to quit each other, an event that would have ripped the social fabric of our high school. No matter how hard they tried, though, they could never bear the loss.

At that time, many of our friends had been calling Brook "Mrs. Davis" for years. Therein lay the embarrassment. Walker was no man of means. The dairy was barely self-sustaining, leaving no flexible income for Grady, much less his son. Walker had always planned on marrying Brook but had not a penny to trade for an engagement ring. Further, he regretted subjecting his beautiful bride to the daily struggle that was dairy farming. He knew in his heart Brook didn't care, but his pride told him the contrary.

"Well, I'll be damned, Walk. I think it's the only logical thing to do with the money, and I'm proud of you. You know I've been waiting for you to tell me this for a decade."

"Whatever, man. I'm telling you now so you can stop giving me hell," he said through a chuckle. "Besides, it won't be this year, with the way the dairy is going."

"No, seriously, I'm excited. I love weddings ... though I guess I've never actually been to one. I love them in theory. Seems like a lot of drinking and dancing—hot girls everywhere." I raised my eyebrows at him.

"Chris, enough—"

"I'll help with the guest list. I can already think of a handful of ladies you need to invite. Let's see, there's Maddy, of course, and Isabelle, and Ashley, and Mary, and—oh—Amy, definitely Amy. Have you set a date yet?"

"I don't even have the r—" He was lost in a game he couldn't win.

"Yes. Absolutely."

"Absolutely *what*?" he shouted, getting more frustrated by the second.

"I'll be your best man, of course!"

Walker simply ceased responding to my comments and banter. This is what he wanted, though. He would prefer I give him a reason to ignore me rather than continue talking about the subject he finally found the courage to broach. I knew him well enough to give him an out. Every great adventure starts with a small step, and this was Walker's. I smiled to myself as I continued processing his words.

We drove the Bronco past the edge of town and turned right onto the highway leading to Highlands. The morning mist was engaged in its slow, deliberate twirls as it bid farewell to the valley streams. We rolled the windows down once we left town to take in the smell of mountain air and the freshly cut grass along the road. It was still too early for most flowers, but the roadside was garnished with early Maypops, soft lavender contrasting against the green of late spring.

As we passed over the second of two small streams, the air suddenly seemed to thicken and move in unexpected ways. Small specks of light yellow and black swarmed above the water and over the bridge. In the absence of foresight, we left the windows down and were soon sharing our vehicle with hundreds of mayflies and stoneflies. While our newfound hitchhikers would have disturbed most, we were giddy to encounter them. Insects mean rising trout, and rising trout means dry-fly fishing. Walker looked at me and grinned like a jackass eating briars, as Grady always said.

At last, we turned off the highway onto the small gravel road leading up to the valley. As was tradition, I extended my hand to the passenger side of the truck, waiting for Walker to give me the ceremonious sign that we were on the last leg of a drive to fish. I felt the cold glass bottle press against my palm, and I took the whiskey from Walker. With one eye watching the road—as if there would be anything to hit—I threw back the bottle and took a long pull. The cold, brown liquid quickly flowed over my tongue and shot down my throat, where it was no longer perceived as cold but rather a tingling burn. I exhaled and tasted fire as I handed the bottle back between bumps in the road.

"Now we're talkin," I said resolutely as I refocused on the road. In these moments, my soul was fully home. I have always loved the act of fly fishing, but something about the morning drives with Walker as we anticipated the day ahead chasing new streams, new trails, and new trout seemed to supersede even the fishing itself. The worries and monotony of life were always left at the turn off the highway. They had no place in the serenity of the mountains. Fly fishing was a sacred and spiritual experience for both me and Walker, and we wouldn't dare stain the clear mountain water with the mire of the outside world. Once we left the highway and felt gravel beneath the tires, nothing else mattered.

We parked at the top of the mountain and quickly located the main trailhead for Lonesome Valley. In those days, we hardly wasted time hiking, especially on the way in to where we were planning to fish; our speed was usually one hair shy of jogging. We trudged down the trail, narrowly avoiding roots that stretched like fingers from large trees, reaching across the path seemingly to grasp their friends on the other side. The ground was soft and richly brown, as it always is during the wet months of the year. The canopy of oak and hickory consisted mostly of smaller leaves still but was complete enough to shield us from the rising sun.

The trail continued to descend from the parking lot until nothing was left to be appreciated of the civilized world. After passing over a trickle of spring water, the dirt path turned again to gravel as the small trail intersected with an old Forest Service road. Following Clyde's directions, we turned left and continued our brisk pace. A series of large switchbacks spanned the broad sloping side of the ancient mountain. At several points along the switchbacks, we noticed small, humble trails disappearing into the woods. Despite knowing they were likely shortcuts, we decided against risking our luck following unmarked paths.

We walked what seemed like a mile of switchbacks only to end a stone's throw from their beginning. The trail was once again soft dirt and stone and had a bubbling creek bordering it to the left. About one hundred steps further, Walker and I stopped to admire a particular tree that seemed to plead for attention. It was a moderately sized eastern white pine that sat on the right side of the trail. Rough layered bark crawled up its trunk and extended out to meet the mottled branches that overhung its base. Most of the branches started around the height of a man, but the left side was barren until about fifteen feet, presumably cut to allow human passage along the trail. Small blue-green needles grew from the end of its slender twigs in bunches of five.

"Everything in the mountains is prettier than it is in the flat country," Walker said, eyes still fixed on the tree. "I'll take an eastern white over a loblolly or shortleaf any day of the week." He walked over and placed his hand on the tree's trunk, as if congratulating it for its very nature.

"Prettier trees, cleaner air, clearer water, but tough to make a living," I responded, not really thinking about my words. Walker made a face but said nothing. "I'm sorry Walk, you know I wasn't talking about—"

"I know. It's fine, it doesn't bother me anyway. I'd rather be poor up here than rich somewhere else." He continued looking at the tree.

"You're looking at that pine like you expect it to say something."

"Well, how do you know it won't? I think if it could talk, it would agree."

I conceded, "Yeah, yeah, it probably would. Now can we please go find some brookies?"

Several paces from the tree, the sound of flowing water began to trickle out of the air and into our ears. The stream we now approached produced different sounds as it coursed over each stone, around each fallen tree, and through every small waterfall. We pursued the symphony of water until we came to a small wooden bridge. Instinctively we both stopped before we reached the old planks, seeing that the water was big enough to hold fish.

"You or me?" Walker said quietly, his voice filled now with the familiar excitement of a fly fisherman on the hunt.

"It's your birthday."

Walker quickly put his fly rod together, peeled line off the reel, passed it through each of the eyes going up the length of the rod, and tied on a small dry fly resembling the insects that filled our car during the morning drive. He then dropped to his hands and knees and slowly crawled to the bridge. I imagined he looked like someone in battle, crawling to the edge of a foxhole to steal a glance at the enemy. He was in his element. He was fly fishing. He had mastered the art over the course of many years and had passionately shared it with me. I was never, and will never be, the fisherman that Walker was, but I didn't care. It was thrilling enough just to watch.

With his head barely high enough to see over the edge, Walker's eyes began methodically picking apart every inch of water under the bridge, in search of pattern, motion, or simply disturbance. A few moments later, his gaze suddenly halted, becoming fixed on a piece of water near the right bank. In a motion as fluid as the water itself, he pointed his rod, pulled the fly line toward his left ear to create tension, and released the line, sending his fly gliding gracefully through the crisp mountain air toward the unsuspecting fish. I had only recently begun to learn bow-and-arrow casts, after years of watching Walker use them. This one was a beauty.

Since I held back several paces from the bridge, I couldn't see the take, but the sound gave it away. A soft splash barely made itself audible above the bubbling of the creek. If one was not anticipating this sound, they would surely have missed it. The hungry brook trout gave little fight, twisting and turning in surrender as Walker stripped in the line. He knelt by the edge of the stream and wet his hands, to protect the fish's outer layer of slime as he gently lifted it from the water. A thin ray of light had broken through the canopy above to brighten the ground on which Walker was sitting, illuminating both my best friend and the colorful fish.

"Well, I guess we broke the skunk," Walker said, referring to the adage about a fishless trip, as he let the fish swim out of his hand and back into his peaceful home.

"The pressure is off," I agreed. "Now we can just have fun!"

The remainder of the morning was one of the best days of fishing I have ever had. After catching the spec under the bridge, we continued shortly down the trail and were greeted for the first time by the beautiful waterfall that would play such a transformative role in both of our lives and in the lives of others. At the time, of course, we were blissfully unaware of its future and were brimming with excitement for this treasure hidden deep in the Appalachian Mountains. Brook trout after brook trout graced our nets and were released back into the clear morning water, each one colored deep green with inlaid speckles of bright orange and pale-blue halos.

Chapter Five

OCTOBER 31, 1983

"WHAT ARE YOU supposed to be? A mall mannequin?" Walker asked as I quite noisily walked toward him on the gravel road leading up to the calf barn. Brook giggled. I looked down at my khaki pants and L. L. Bean jacket.

"I thought you only dressed up for Halloween if you were twelve years old, or the mother of a twelve-year-old," I responded dully. Truth be told, I never liked to be overdressed, underdressed, or in this case maybe improperly dressed. As I looked back and forth from Walker to Brook, dressed as Shaggy and Daphne, respectively, I felt embarrassed that I hadn't received the costume memo.

"Who invited this Halloweenie?" Daphne asked, shivering, as Shaggy walked into the barn, obviously searching for something. Brook lacked the insulation of excess weight. She was a skinny five and a half feet tall, with deep walnut-brown eyes that matched her hair. She was objectively beautiful. In fact, I have always believed she was the prettiest girl in Transylvania County in those days. Everything about her was delicate and dainty, as if God had picked the finest tools to craft her. Of course, tonight she wore a purple dress with a green scarf. Her long, fair legs were covered in light-pink hose. Now, feeling satisfied in her costume reveal, she pulled on her wool jacket.

"Look, if you wanted me to dress up just to drink whiskey around a bonfire, you should've said something. Besides, aren't Daphne and Fred supposed to go together? He looks an awful lot like Shaggy."

Brook looked toward the barn to make sure Walker was out of hearing range before frowning. "That's exactly what I told him, but he wouldn't hear it. 'I relate more to Shaggy' he said. 'Fred is a yuppie, et cetera, et cetera.' You know Walk."

Walker returned with some blue hay twine and a yellow cattle ear tag. After passing the twine through a hole in the tag he tied it around my neck. "Now you can be Scooby." Brook gave an approving look. "Anyway ... just drink whiskey? Who said anything about just drinking whiskey?" Walker reached into his jeans and pulled out a bag labeled Scooby Snacks.

"Ah, I see," I retorted as Walker pulled out three brownies.

"Do we have to do something spooky to earn them, or can we just eat them?"

"One for Daphne, one for me, and last but not least, one for Scooby-Doo." Walker added extra emphasis to my "name" as he handed us our brownies.

I smelled my brownie and was satisfied to find it smelled like chocolate, and nothing more. The same could likely not be said for Walker's and Brook's brownies.

"Is there any chocolate in these?" asked Brook as she pretended to wretch.

"Halloween only comes once a year," Walker responded.

"Great. If we're lucky, we will make it to the next one," I added.

I never judged Walker for his use of marijuana, but I had made the moral decision at a young age to never partake. One of the worst fights Walker and I had ever gotten into was in high school when he snuck weed into a piece of chocolate, he had given me. By the time I realized what happened, my body was starting to feel unnaturally heavy, and the world moved in slow-motion. When I confronted Walker about it, he got defensive and called me a slang term for a certain part of female anatomy. That threw me over the edge. What started as a light-hearted prank commenced to an all-out brawl, leaving us both bloodied and in need of new clothes. After sleeping our anger off, we awoke the next day and never spoke of it again. Walker never tried giving me marijuana again.

Walker, in those days, was a pothead. I knew it, Brook knew it, Grady probably even knew it. No one seemed to care, since all it did was make him kind and mellow. Brook used to partake on occasion, but often refused, weighing risk and reward for her future. Halloween night in 1983 she partook.

"Zoinks!" Walker said as he gobbled his brownie.

"Creepers!"

"Scooby-Dooby-Doo." I rolled my eyes but nevertheless ate my share. "Now what? I asked. "We only have an hour before we need to be on a couch."

"Glad you asked! Follow me," Walker said.

Our party of three meddling kids was now walking past the calf barn and toward the milking parlor. We stopped inside to grab a couple of beers from our secret stash in the back of the colostrum refrigerator.

The cold liquid coursed down the back of my tongue and into my belly, where it summoned a noticeable chill. It wasn't unusually cold outside, but I was typically not wandering around a farm drinking Coors at night in late October. Forty-five degrees cuts through clothes much faster when it's penetrating you from the outside in and the inside out.

We continued our stroll past the main barn and toward the larger of two equipment sheds. The milking herd must have been alerted by our footsteps, as some of the cows began to groan. I caught sight of a young Holstein who was previously sleeping near the food trough. She was mostly black, so much so that she could have been confused for an Angus cow if it weren't for her size and the more angular shape of her face. As we approached, her large head turned to look at us, and she began the laborious process of standing up. Her back hooves contacted the wet concrete first, and she hoisted her hindquarters skyward. Next were her elbows, pressing firmly into the mix of sand and manure beneath her. She struggled to turn over her front hooves and finally hoisted her body in its entirety.

She tilted back her head and bellowed into the cold night, her voice both audible and visible. As the moisture from within her met the bitter October air, it created a fog of breath that poured from her mouth and both nostrils. At the same time, a cool breeze flooded down the mountainside through the trees, bringing a flutter of leaves over our heads.

At last, we came to a halt past the shed. Grady's new baby-blue Ford 1200 tractor was sitting out from under the shed, attached to a small flatbed trailer. On the trailer were several bales of straw, stacked neatly along the edges.

"A hayride!" Brook exclaimed, realizing now the plan for the evening.

"Climb on up, I've got something to show you." Walker slung himself up to the steering wheel as we climbed onto the trailer, taking a seat on the firm bales.

He turned the engine over, and the powerful little tractor sighed a billow of black smoke from the exhaust pipe. The smell of decaying fall leaves was soon replaced by the scent of a working farm—oil and grease. We held on to the scratchy bales of hay as Walker engaged the clutch.

"Where are we going?" I shouted to Walker, as the trailer lurched forward toward the back of the far-off pasture and the edge of the trees that climbed into the sky like resolute silhouetted giants. Walker either didn't hear me or wanted to keep it a secret and thus never responded. I looked toward Brook, asking her the same question by raising my eyebrows in her direction.

"Beats me." She was briefly illuminated by the delicate rays of the moon, escaping from the clouds high above. Her gaze robbed you of your dignity. She had a habit of maintaining eye contact longer than most, forcing you to finally look away first for fear of teetering on the fine edge between acknowledgment and passion. Of course, entirely innocent and naive, she had this effect on everyone. Only Walker had allowed it to push past the point of no return. I loved Brook dearly and would have truly died for her, but I never loved her as more than a sister. Nevertheless, I turned my gaze back toward Walker, who was bouncing up and down at the tractor's helm, smiling to himself, enjoying the company of friends on this late-night adventure.

The tractor lumbered on, and we passed into the woods that, unbeknownst to us, would one day be part of the Pisgah National Forest. The trail, too narrow for the tractor that pulled the TMR wagon, was just wide enough for the smaller 1200. The headlights met the tall wooden giants and cast long shadows ahead of us that shortened and disappeared to our sides as we continued along the dirt path.

We continued like this for some time. My thoughts began to twirl around in my brain, through every nook and cranny.. I thought of what Walker had told me on his birthday that year, about the engagement ring. I wondered if he had looked for one yet. He had a frustrating habit of letting things dwell and eventually stale. Mine and Brook's world was changing daily as we considered our futures. Our time in the mountains could be coming to an end if no clear path was laid out before us. Walker seemed stuck out of the realm of space and time. He existed as a dairy farmer seemingly in his own universe and hadn't stopped long enough to consider the rest of us had to make plans.

Realizing I was staring silently at the wooden planks of the trailer, I lifted my head to see how Brook was doing. Eyes glazed over, she leaned against a hay bail and stared out into the dark of night. Her mind was probably numbing.

The shadows seemed to reach out and touch the black of the forest now, as if the forest was sending tendrils of darkness to pull us in. At some point while I was deep in thought, Brook had laid down on her back and was watching the clouds pass over the moon. An almost skunklike smell passed over me in a cloud of smoke. I looked toward Walker, who exhaled another fragrant cloud before extinguishing the little joint on the side of the metal tractor and flicking the remains onto the trail. I watched it bounce twice before coming to rest next to the trailer. I tried to keep my eyes fixed on it as we continued moving forward, until it finally extended beyond the reach of my vision into the dark night.

How many people had looked at this same moon for hundreds—no, thousands—of years? I thought mostly of the Cherokee, who had lived here not long before we did. I remembered reading stories of these Indians camping on mountain knobs, fishing for the same brook trout that captured our imaginations. I wonder if they would have accepted me and Walker as one of them. Language barriers broken by the chase for these little colorful fish. We could teach them to fly fish, and they could share their tobacco pipes with us in small lodges.

As I looked around, I thought of the stories these trees would tell if they *could* talk. Maybe they could talk. I wondered if it was merely mankind's fault for not being fluent in the subtle voices of nature that came dripping through the ether all around us. At that moment, another breeze came swirling through the forest and gently passed through my body. For a brief second, I thought I heard voices in the wind. Wait, why could I hear anything over the sound of the tractor?

"To be honest, I thought you would both be more impressed." The voice was Walker's. At some point while I was exploring rabbit holes in my mind, I had laid down, enjoying the subtle buzz of the beer and longcut tobacco. Both Brook and I sat up and noticed the tractor was off. We had arrived. Walker's voice had pulled me from my thoughts and into the present. I noticed we were in a clearing deep in the woods.

"It's perfect, Walk! This is what you've been working on all fall."

"Damn, Walker," I said as I looked around at the quarter-acre opening. I climbed down from the trailer and strolled towards Walker, who was now sitting on a stump near a fire ring. Brook was shortly behind me but moving at a much slower and more effortful pace. We all sat around the ring together while Walker struck a match and began lighting the tinder. Clearly his tolerance for marijuana was higher than Brook's. I was happy to be of sound mind in these moments.

Nature was spiritual for both Walker and me, but we experienced it differently. In my mind, just existing in these moments deep in the woods made me feel close to my creator. The brush strokes of God were laid upon the canvas of Appalachia in a way that made it impossible not to notice. I believe Walker felt the same way, but he added an extra layer of mysticism with mind-altering drugs. He described himself as being spiritually connected to the trees, the water, and even the wind. I tried to tell him he didn't need drugs to experience that, but he smoked anyway.

I inhaled a deep breath of fresh, cool autumn. The oaks, hemlocks, and pines around the edge of the clearing seemed like walls of a castle. With each passing cloud, you could just make out the dark green of the hemlock needles and the brown of the leaves at our feet. Soon, tiny flames were licking the night air, and Walker leaned back away from the ring. We sat for several moments, listening to the gentle pops and whistles of the fire. *Are these noises the painful groanings of the trees we burn?* I didn't like that thought.

"This is awesome. It's like our own little kingdom back here, away from the rest of the world."

"It's just for us," Walker responded to Brook.

"Forever, right?" I asked.

Walker looked at me in a way that said now was forever and forever was now.

A healthy fire was steadily burning now, and the hissing of trapped water was replaced by a steady crackling of dry wood. I thought again of the trees and their voices. *Stop it.*

"Are y'all as thirsty as I am?" Walker uncorked a bottle of Jack Daniel's and passed it to Brook. "Ladies first."

"Do ladies drink whiskey from the bottle?" Brook asked.

"Mine does."

Smiling, Brook took a long pull from the bottle and exhaled deeply. "I'll be honest, I'm feeling quite fuzzy on the inside."

I took the bottle next and began drinking, as I made eye contact with Brook, raised my eyebrows, and nodded in agreement. I was doing my best to catch up with long, strong pulls from the bottle.

"Let's tell ghost stories," Walker said.

"Noooo, I get too scared, Walker. I'm not as comfortable in the woods at night as you are. And your stories are always so spooky." Brook tried her best but to no avail.

"You know this used to be a burial ground many years ago, and—"

"Ugh!" Brook grunted. I laughed under my breath.

"—and in those days, smallpox had begun to ravage the native people of these mountains. Having no immunity, it ran through them like fire, rotting the flesh off their faces. It would make boils in their throats and drip nasty fluid down into their lungs, slowly suffocating them."

"Jesus, Walker," I now said, in support of Brook, who was grimacing.

"Hold on, it gets better," he said, smiling. "The tribe had shrunk to about half of its original size, and its boundaries shrank away from this area further into the woods, leaving the dead to wither away from the company of their living relatives."

He continued, "A white family, looking for a place to farm, moved into the valley and took advantage of the now-empty forest. They established a small homestead right at the base of this mountain, near what's now the far-off pasture."

At this, I started paying closer attention, since there was an old, abandoned cabin rotting in the corner of the Davises' far-off pasture.

"Initially their encounters with the natives were scarce, since they had assumed contact with white people was spreading smallpox. The only interactions they had were warnings to stay out of the forest. One day, however, the young children of the farmers, one boy and one girl, wandered into the woods."

Brook shifted uneasily in her seat.

"The story goes—remember there were no witnesses for this part—that the children started to hear voices, whispers laced in the wind, calling them deeper into the forest until they arrived at the very spot where we now sit. The closer they got, the more the whispers seemed to leave the wind and crawl out of the ground beneath them."

My eyes were glued to Walker now. His expressions intensified as the story continued and he touched the forest floor. "What happened?" I asked.

"They walked home hand in hand, out of the woods."

"Wait, that's it?" asked Brook, partially relieved.

"Oh no. They walked home, but they were changed. When their parents found them at the back door of the cabin, their eyes were milked over, pupilless, and they were speaking in a tongue not known to the white settlers. They were breathing in wet, raspy gasps as if they were choking. Thinking they were ill, their parents gave them each a dollop of cough syrup and put them to bed."

"Around midnight, the two parents were awoken by the sound of gagging and nails scratching down the thin door separating the two rooms of the small cabin."

"Walker, this story better be over soon. I really don't like this," Brook said, as her face grew pale.

"When the county sheriff hadn't heard from the family after about a week, he sent a deputy to check on the farm. The smell of death met him when he reached the last step leading up to the porch. He passed through the open door and found two adult bodies, almost unrecognizable. They had been stabbed numerous times, and their scalps were missing. But worse than that, they were both completely skinned. Blood stained the floor beneath them."

Walker's voice was now frantic. "Thinking immediately that the natives had been involved, he gathered a small posse to go with him into the woods to their known burial site. When they arrived at this spot, they stopped and fell to their knees. From the branch in that sycamore ..." he said as he pointed to a tree on the edge of the clearing, "two small bodies hung, skin mustard yellow. Unmistakable, they were the farmer's children. Eyes were white and their jaws were unhinged. The sheriff finally got to his feet, eyes wet, and started walking toward the base of the tree. When he was only ten feet from the trunk, the midday sky suddenly went black, and the two bodies lifted their arms and pointed to the sheriff ... '*Death!*'" Walker screamed this last word with a throaty vigor that made both me and Brook jump. I fell off the stump and knocked my breath away, causing me to start gasping.

"Walker, I *hate* you!" Brook yelled at him. "Damn it, I'm not going to sleep for weeks." At this point, Walker was laughing so hard he could barely breathe.

"Hahaha you chicken shits, you should have seen your faces. Chris, did you get bucked off your seat?"

"Wait, shut up, Walker," I said as I regained my composure. "What was that?"

Brook now looked like she might wet her pants. Sure enough, something was rustling in the leaves of the very same sycamore from Walker's story. Now it was the storyteller's turn to be scared. Walker stood up and grabbed us both by the arm and ran us to the trailer. We jumped over the front edge and lay silently between the bales of straw. The noise grew louder. The sound of nails on bark was now unmistakable. The creature seemed to be moving down the tree toward the ground. When the leaves of the forest floor started shuffling, Brook grabbed one of our hands in each of hers. She squeezed tight enough to make me wince.

"Ghosts aren't real, ghosts aren't real, ghosts aren't real ..." I heard her whispering to herself. I didn't believe in ghosts either, but I was starting to rethink my beliefs. The leaves continued to scatter in a pattern that could only mean one thing—whatever we were hearing was coming for the trailer.

"Son of a bitch!" I shouted as I felt bravery and a desperate desire to protect my best friends well up from my heart. I quickly shot up to my feet to confront the beast. What I saw sent me into a fit of laughter.

"May I present the eastern gray squirrel," I said loudly. The squirrel, no doubt coming to see who was disturbing his sleep, was now more scared than we were and darted quickly back to the tree and the safety of his nest.

Walker resumed laughing and sat up against one of the straw bales. Brook closed her eyes and sighed with relief while also sitting up. I sat down on the other side of Walker, who put his arms around us.

Once the panic-turned-hilarity wore off, we sat in silence for what seemed like an hour. Brook broke the silence. "I suppose we are to believe the story was about your ancestors or something?"

"Um, how would I be here if it were about my ancestors?" Walker responded.

"Oh, I guess that's a good point. Do you believe any of that stuff you make up stories about, Walk?"

"I believe there are whispers on the wind. But I don't think it's no Indian ghosts. I think the mountains talk to the rivers and trees, and I think they talk back."

"Do you think we can hear them?"

"That's for you to ask yourself."

"I hear them," I said. "At least I think I hear them. They're faint, but there if you let your soul be quiet long enough to listen."

Walker silently nodded.

"Are they good or evil?" Brook asked.

"They aren't good or evil. They just are. It's the people that are good and evil."

"But what do you think they w—"

"Just be quiet and listen," I interrupted.

We lay there the rest of the night, riding the fine line between asleep and awake, listening to the wind swirl in the canopy. The dread of the evening was gone, and we were all at peace. As we leaned against one another, hoping to hear the voices of the mountains, the rivers, and the trees, I remember wondering why moments like that had to ever end. We were as much a part of the forest as the plants and animals, and we were also a part of each other. *What would I do without these two?* I thought as I drifted to sleep.

Chapter Six

JUNE 15, 1984

PAUL ANDERSON WRIGHT. That name would eventually bring our little mountain town to its knees, but in the summer of '84, it was entirely unknown. It first presented itself to me on the afternoon of June 15, while I sipped coffee on Brook Palmer's front porch.

That day I was exhausted after spending the morning at the paper mill, as had become habit that summer. Most of my friends from school had found jobs as rafting guides, interns at the fish hatchery, or employees at hiking stores in nearby Highlands. I, however, had been pressured by my father to spend the humid days of summer toiling in an unbearably hot plant. "It will add valuable experience to your resume, Chris," he had said. At least the miserable work was counterbalanced by decent pay. Regardless, I was too tired to put up much of a fight when Brook asked me for a massive favor.

"What's the worst that could happen, Chris? I'm not asking you to be his best friend, though we all know you and Walker *need* more friends. I just think you would like him, and he doesn't know a soul up here. Take him fishing once. For me ... please?"

I knew I couldn't resist her pleading brown eyes, so I focused on the light-blue porch ceiling, a relic of Mr. Palmer's Charlestonian past. "People transfer to Brevard every semester, Brook. Why is it so important to you that we make friends with ... what's his name again?" I slumped forward in the chair and rested my chin in my interlocked hands.

"Paul. Paul Wright. And it's because my father knows him, well kind of. He knows his Pa. Dr. Wright wrote to Daddy, asking if we could try to introduce Paul to some of our friends. You know how different the mountains are from Charleston."

"Yeah, and I thank God for it daily." In a moment of weakness, my eyes met hers, and it was over. "Okay, fine. One time. If he's at all what I'm expecting, it will be the only time."

"Yay! Thank you, Chris, I owe you. You're going to love him anyway."

Brook turned her head toward the road and smiled in humble victory, her brown waves gently fluttering in the breeze of the approaching spring shower. She wore a light-gray, loosely fitting College of Charleston pullover and faded jeans. I can't imagine anyone else was wearing a jacket that June afternoon, but Brook was always cold. Her legs were currently rested upon the railing of the porch, its paint a parched and flaking white.

"Why don't you ask Walker these kinds of things?" I asked her, though I already knew the answer. My relationship with Brook was as deep as the friendship I shared with Walker but entirely different. Since her father took to the bottle, I had become her protector, her comforter, and her confidant. Walker, of course, as her boyfriend held many of those titles nominally and had for years, yet it was me who carried out the labors that such titles bestowed. We rarely talked of their relationship, as I felt that was unfair to my best friend. We did, however, talk about everything else. We talked of her father and his struggle with alcoholism, we talked of our classes at college, we discussed the drama of our town, and we reminisced on a simpler time before the world forced adulthood on us.

Brook needed someone outside of her romantic relationship who would always be there for her. Someone whose emotions were not interwoven with hers. Someone who viewed her as family but not with a longing heart. Such a person could weather the storms of her life and respond with whatever encouragement she so dearly needed, with solely her interests at heart.

Brook's eyes dramatically rolled in their sockets as she looked back toward me. "You know Walker." She then did an uncannily accurate impression of her boyfriend, lowering her voice, layering it with a thick southern twang. "'I'm not ruining the beauty of fly fishing with some fancy Charleston doctor wannabe.' He'll listen to you, though." She was right, and I knew it. The only way Paul would fish with us was if the idea originated from me, and so it did.

Two days later, at about eight fifteen in the morning, Walker and I waited on the front steps of the Palmers' porch and listened to the mountains awaken. Most of the day would be clear and sunny, but a gentle morning shower, not much more than a mist, was currently wetting the forest around Brook and her father's home. Several squirrels moved through the woods in front of the house, beginning to gather food for the distant winter, barking every now and then when they noticed us. Something larger broke a branch behind the house, causing the squirrels to dart up an oak in alarm.

"Why are we meeting him here?" Walker asked me in a subdued grumble, breaking the serene rhythm of the rain hitting the canopy. He turned and faced me with a bored expression. He was certainly not looking forward to giving anyone lessons today. He also made no effort to hide any of his emotions. If Walk was bored, you knew it.

"I think he came by here a few weeks ago when he moved, since his family knows the Palmers from Charleston. His father is a doctor down there and knew Mr. Palmer when he was in law school. I think they were pretty good friends. Both Brook and Paul were born the year after the Palmers left Charleston. Dr. Wright hoped they could meet each other and that she could introduce him to some of her guy friends."

"Hm. And he's starting at Brevard this year?"

"Yep, studying science, I guess. He wants to go to medical school after college, presumably back at MUSC in Charleston. He did his first three years of undergrad at College of Charleston but apparently wanted to see somewhere else for his last year."

"I can't say I blame him, but I don't see why we have to take him fishing. Does he even know how to fish?" Walker stared at the ground by his feet, in annoyed contemplation. In all my years of knowing him, he never had a lot of friends. He was hardheaded, and his personality was not well restrained, but his lonesomeness was largely by choice. He toiled long hours, had a relationship that seemed eternal, and was insatiably bored by most of our peers. He was passionate through and through. He could not withstand hours of small talk and never tolerated drama or gossip. Walker could never understand the lack of energy in most people's souls, the lack of appreciation for the world around them, and the utter dullness of words that they wasted breath on. Hence, he was left with me and Brook, neither of whom fit those exclusive qualifications. Apprehension painted his face while he thought of our wishful low-country friend.

"Brook said he's been practicing in a field," I responded, trying not to laugh.

"Great."

We continued in silence for a while. The clouds were getting thinner by the minute, and the rain had moved on, in search of another place to fall. The guttural voice of a V8 engine came galloping down Brook's driveway as a spotless red Camaro turned the corner and made its way toward us, slinging gravel and leaving a billowing trail of dust behind it.

"You can't make this shit up," Walker said, seemingly to himself.

"It's a Z28 too. Looks like Mommy and Daddy's money," I responded.

The car stopped at the base of the steps, hood steaming from evaporating rain, and out stepped our new companion. "I'm Paul," the figure said, smiling. Standing just shy of six feet, topped with freshly combed dirty-blond hair, Paul was handsome and knew it. His skin was darkened from the early summer in the low country, and the sun had gifted his face with small constellations of freckles. The shape of his nose, and moreover his overall facial structure, seemed sculpted. His jawline was resolute, and his lips were parted to reveal a perfect white smile, a rare sight for the simple country folk of the southern Appalachian Mountains. His eyes, as expected, were a vivid light blue. Athleticism emanated from his figure, which was muscular and lean. His clothes also helped paint the picture of our first impression. He wore a lightweight blue fishing shirt, expensive forest-green pants, and was adorned with gear of the highest quality. His vest alone probably cost him more than my and Walker's rods. Paul was the epitome of money married to good genes. Despite all these reasons for initial disdain, his smile disarmed us both.

"Mornin'," I responded as Paul walked toward the steps, hand extended.

"Howdy, Paul," Walker added. "Ever been fly fishing before?"

"Nope. I've been practicing casting for a few weeks, though, and I've read a couple books." He laughed nervously.

"It's the only hobby you'll ever need. I'm Walker, and this is Chris," he said, nodding toward me. We both shook our new acquaintance's hand firmly. Walker's eyes studied Paul, trying to find a weakness or a character flaw of some sort. He so dearly longed for a reason not to take him with us.

I have been Baptist my whole life, spending Sundays in church since before my brain started holding on to memories. Walker's religion, on the other hand, was trout fishing. His hymns were the sound of a mountain breeze through the morning pine needles. His communion with God took place deep in the valleys of Southern Appalachia. I would often hear him or see him talking gently while he fished. To Walker, God spoke through nature, not in some wooden building constructed by the cultural elite. God was in the morning mist, the cool flowing water, the warming rays of sun, and in the movement of mountain air. Thus, fishing was not just a hobby for my best friend. It was a spiritual journey shared only with me and his Maker.

After not finding anything blatantly wrong with the guy, Walker finally said, "All right, well let's do it, then," and we loaded into the Bronco.

This morning we decided to fish the near-by Davidson. Easily accessible and known to all, the Davidson was filled with smart, if not wary, trout that have seen every fly known to man and likely have been caught by most of them at some point. Sore mouths remind them of their past mistakes, and they generally laugh at you when you try to catch them. The perfect place for a beginner—or so we told Paul.

As the truck turned off the highway onto the forest service road adjacent to the river, Paul spoke up from the back seat. "So, Walker, Mr. Palmer tells me you and Brook are in a relationship?"

"That's right."

"If you'd have asked that question a decade ago, the answer would be the same," I added.

Walker rolled his eyes as he handed Paul the bottle of whiskey. Paul stared back at him, obviously confused.

"It's tradition. We've turned off the highway," I explained.

"When in Rome, I guess." Paul uncorked the bottle and took a short pull. The first sign of distress was in his eyes. Until that point collected and confident, his blue eyes now narrowed, and his pupils seemed to shrink. Next was the tightening of his abdomen and the resulting contortion of his posture.

Oh no, I thought, in the brief moment between alarm and disaster.

He grabbed the back of Walker's seat to brace for the coming wretch. It started as a dry cough but quickly turned for the worst. On his third wretch, he rebirthed the Jack Daniel's onto the back of my passenger seat.

It's not that I didn't try; I really did. However, the moment got the best of me. My eyes also began to narrow, my abdomen clenched, and I braced the steering wheel. What came out of my mouth, however, was not whiskey or vomit, but rather a muffled, struggling laugh. Walker, at seeing my response, began to chuckle as well. He turned and looked out the window to try to control himself.

"I don't drink liquor very often," Paul managed to get out, in not much more than a defeated whisper, mouth still wet from his exorcism.

"You don't say," Walker said through laughter, as he turned and looked at him.

Minutes later, after parking and briefly cleaning up the back seat, the Bronco was empty and alone on the side of the winding road while we picked our way through the dense green vegetation that lined every stream during the warm, humid summer months. The sweet sound of cold mountain water called us down the bank like the sirens of old mythology.

"This here, this is heaven." I felt my lips move as the words subconsciously flowed from my mouth. My eyes met Paul's, and I noticed something that changed my perspective on this newly met stranger. Walker and I had begrudgingly "taught" many of our friends how to fish. Most of them had little real interest and never experienced the emotional magic that kept us coming back. They wanted to like it, but they missed the point. Fishing wasn't the addiction; it was the setting.

Something about the subtle, wet twinkle in Paul's eyes made my heart pause. I knew that look. His eyes mirrored mine when Walker first took me. The thought that twirled and tossed through my thoughts the rest of the day between casts and fish was *Maybe the kid just needs a chance*.

"You're a natural!" Walker called across the stream to a kneeling Paul, who had just netted the first trout of his life after only thirty minutes of casting. His arms were quivering as he gently raised the small rainbow out of its home and into ours.

"It's a bow!" Walker was wading—no, running—across the stream, awkwardly raising one leg at a time as high from the water as his height would allow. I quickly followed suit, though a couple inches taller and with longer legs, I made easier work of the waist-high river. Two-thirds of the way across, Walker took a bad step and entered the underwater ecosystem mouth first. I was nearly caught up to him at this point and grabbed his waders from behind, lifting him back to his feet.

"Hey man, I think it drops off there," I yelled in passing while I made my way to the opposite bank, where Paul still clutched his prize. Walker had begun laughing as his head breached the surface, resulting in a spew of mountain water that any onlooker may have perceived as drowning.

"Look at those colors! That's a beaut', Paul! See the green spots and bright-red side? He's colored up perfect for your first trout." Walker was beaming over Paul's fish while I stood next to them, lips pulled back as if by a puppeteer revealing a smile that only fishing brought me.

"This is amazing. I've never felt a rush like this. I was worried I was going to lose him when he started jumping. Are they all this pretty?"

"Yeah man, but we gotta get you a brookie. Those are the real gems of Appalachia," Walker responded emphatically. It was happening, and it was faster than I could have ever predicted. Something about Paul's raw excitement in the stream had led to Walker deciding he liked him, and there were few people Walker liked.

"I'll go any day of the week," said our new friend.

Walker, Paul, and I fished the remainder of the day, only stopping to sip bourbon and eat packs of crackers, our standard angling cuisine. The overcast morning gave rise to a clear, breezy afternoon, clouds elongated by the prevailing winds from soft pillows into thin strips, before finally being welcomed back into the stratosphere. The air did its best to guide Paul's line into the overhanging rhododendron, but the infant fly fisherman beat nature more times than not. Whether he was a natural or merely had cast ten thousand lines in his "field" was never determined, but at this point, it didn't matter. We were fishing, and Paul held his own.

When I got home that evening, well after sundown, I collapsed on the living room couch and started reorganizing my fly box. Paul had purchased a dozen flies prior to our outing, meaning he had maybe one or two that were appropriate for that time of year. Because of that, I ended up giving him full access to my inventory of several hundred flies, nymphs, and streamers. Walker always made it very clear only I could use his flies, since he spent hours hand-tying each and every one of them. Mine were merely store bought and I didn't have the same emotional attachment.

"Chris, how many times must I tell you? *Please* get your sandy behind off the couch! You can sit on our furniture after you shower, not before!"

"Okay, okay Mom."

"How did today go, anyway?" she pressed. "How was it meeting a new friend? Remind me his name again?"

"Paul," I responded as I closed my biggest fly box and stood up off the old, cracked leather couch, wondering why it was so important to keep the monstrosity clean. "It went well. I like him. More importantly, I think Walker really liked him. It's not always easy to tell with him, but his complaining was less than the last time we took a new 'friend.'"

"That's wonderful! You need more friends. Walker has been such a great friend all these years, but you can't only have one."

"I assume you are just forgetting about Brook?" I asked dully.

"No, I am not *forgetting* about Brook. What I mean is you need more guy friends. One of these days, Brook and Walker are going to get married and probably have a family. You need someone to hang out with when that happens, or else you'll just have to spend time with your demanding old mother," she said, smiling. She walked over and put her arms around my shoulders. "I know how horrible *that* would be for you."

"Oh stop, Mom. I know, I know. What do you want me to say? I'm trying." *Thanks to you and Brook*, I thought.

She gave me a kiss on the forehead and stepped away. "You better get some sleep. Your father wants you at the plant first thing tomorrow morning. There is a big order that needs filling."

"Ugh," I moaned, thinking of the long day ahead.

Chapter Seven

SUMMER 1984

THE REMAINDER OF that summer, apart from when I was at work, was pure, raw happiness and thus fleeting. The longest days of the year seemed as short as the passing afternoon showers that dropped their life-giving rain on the deep-green, rolling landscape. Our intimate group of companions had grown by one. What started with a small rainbow trout in mid-June blossomed with the wildflowers into a real friendship.

Paul Wright was one of us now, though not to say he didn't have his differences. He was obviously not from the mountains, and his previous life in Charleston hadn't prepared him for this new setting. His pace was very hurried compared to mine, Brook's, and Walker's. He ran through each day with objectives and plans. He tried to make everything productive, and thus we were often forced to slow him down. Walker and I were not lazy, but the pace in the hills is slower than the flatland. Sure, we had objectives, but years had taught us to appreciate the beauty of every moment, from the shapes of clouds to the color of trees. With our help, Paul was learning, though not without growing pains.

Paul also spoke more of money than we did, which is not unexpected from someone whose parents are both practicing physicians. He wasn't overbearing by any means, but passing comments often resulted in my eyes meeting Walker's, both minds wishing he would live in his own moment and not through his parents' success. We both believed the perfect amount of money is just enough to get by, staving off financial stress. Any more than that would start stripping you of your freedom and dull your appreciation of the world.

In general, though, Paul was a fun person to be around. He had an energy like Walker's. The next grand adventure lay around every corner, the biggest fish was in the next stream, and the best was always yet to come. People like that capture your spirit. It was always hard to have bad days around Walker and Paul. Optimism lit up the world around them like the rays of the morning sun.

On a particularly cool evening in late July, the result of a front the day before, the four of us sat on blankets in a field. The movie being projected on the large screen had lost our interest not long after it started. We were far enough from other onlookers to be able to converse freely. Walker sat upright against a large stump and was running his fingers through Brook's wavy brown hair. Brook, wearing faded jeans and a green fleece, was lying on her back, head in Walker's lap. Paul and I sat opposite the two lovers, backs to the movie.

"Don't be such a stubborn ass! Everyone knows she likes you. It's basically all she talks about. Trust me, the only one keeping you single is you." Brook was currently berating me about my indecisiveness with Maddy, who happened to be her best friend. Maddy was everything I wanted in a woman. Her cascading blonde hair, her smooth bronze skin, her melodious laugh. We were friends, but mostly through Brook. I had been debating asking her on a date for over six months but couldn't find the courage.

"Okay, okay. What if I ask her to the Fall Formal? Would that make you all happy?" I responded.

"Yes!" the three voices shouted back at me in unison.

"Although girls do tend to tie you down," Walker said thoughtfully, lowering his chin to look at Brook.

She rolled her eyes and abruptly sat up, "What are we doing here? I want to have funnn. We've seen this movie a hundred times, and I'm bored!"

Ignoring Brook, Paul looked at me and asked, "Where are we ripping lips tomorrow?"

"You know I hate that phrase. We aren't fishing with treble hooks like some flatland neanderthal. Fly fishing is *graceful*, and we certainly aren't trying to 'rip lips,'" Walker grumbled at Paul.

"Walk, should we take him to Lonesome Valley?" I looked at my best friend, who had gotten up to grab another beer. His answer came as two cold cans, one flying to me and the other bouncing off Paul's hand before hitting the dirt.

"Only if Paul catches the next one." The next beer came flying as soon as the words left Walker's mouth. Paul stood up for this one and used both hands, watching it the whole way in, as if he were playing catcher. This can did not hit the dirt. "It's settled then. We'll fish the valley."

"Hey, that's great and all ... but what are we doing *tonight*?" pleaded Brook, her eyes piercing all our souls as they bounced from one man to the next.

Realizing Brook's mood would shortly transition from fun begging to sour indifference, Walker responded, "Who wants to break the law?"

After driving back down Main Street, the four of us mocking tourists polluting the local restaurants and stores, we turned on a small road that led to the back of town toward the old water tower. I turned the headlights off as we pulled in behind the chain fence. After looking in all directions, we piled out of the Bronco and quietly approached the obsolete giant.

"Ladies first," Walker said, grabbing Brook's waist and hoisting her up toward the top of the fence. Luckily the county hadn't yet noticed the clipped section of barbed wire. Paul climbed next, followed by me in the rear. In those days, the ladder extended all the way to the ground, making the climb to the small landing at the top fairly simple. Although, carrying beer cans complicated the ascent quite a bit. Nevertheless, one by one we all finally pushed off the final rung and pulled ourselves onto the metal deck that extended out from the circumference of the tank.

"Wow." Paul broke the silence, his eyes fixed to the horizon. When I looked at him, his face was illuminated with soft orange and pink. Before us lay the town of Brevard, all visible in one small quarter of our panorama. The headlights of cars were lazily passing through town, and people shuffled along the sidewalks. Sweet smoke rose from the barbecue restaurant and was caught in an eastern breeze that gently carried the aroma of brisket and pulled pork toward the water tower.

Paul, however, was not moved to words by the smells of Appalachian cuisine or by the sights of the town. In that moment, what captured us all was the scene above Brevard. The succession of blue ridges started with the mountain that bordered our valley, deep and darkly blue, and continued far into the summer horizon. Each subsequent mountain was a lighter shade and less defined, until finally the most distant peaks melted into the sky, giving only the illusion of structure. There was something almost ghastly about the colors, shapes, and fading definition of the distant reaching giants.

A descending orange light, only a sliver left in our world, was bleeding the sky around the horizon. Dense, impermeable red was draped on the intersection of sky and hill, extending from the sun outward in all directions.

Legs dangling over the platform, we sat in silence for several minutes, only looking away to take sips from the cold cans of cheap beer. Walker reached into the front pocket of his red-and-black plaid flannel and pulled out a small plastic bag and a smooth glass pipe. He quietly packed the loose green mixture into a depression at the end of the glass.

"Does anyone have a light?" he asked when finished. I tossed him a small lighter and looked back at the setting sun. A gentle crackling burn was followed by a soft exhalation and the smell of familiar, comforting smoke. He passed it first to Brook, who pulled in a soft stream of smoke and smiled at no one in particular. Paul, not unsurprisingly, struggled about as much as he did with the whiskey. The more he tried to suppress his cough, the worse it became. After a particularly rough series of gagging, he finally gathered his composure. I looked past him at Walker, who rolled his eyes.

"Are you a lunger?" I asked Paul, who looked away in embarrassment.

"A what? I don't know what that means," he responded.

"A lunger. You know, someone with tuberculosis?"

"Do you want any?" he asked, ignoring my question, as he started to hand the pipe to me.

"I'm good. You've ruined my appetite. For the record, you're supposed to smoke from the pipe, not French kiss it."

"Chris is a weenie," Brook said, looking at Paul. "He's too good to smoke."

"Don't start with that, Brook," Walker said in my defense. "Chris can do whatever the hell he wants. He's still here with us, isn't he?"

Silence and darkness descended upon our party, as we watched the last rays of light concede to the cool mountain evening. Subtle moon shadows passed over the distant hillsides across the valley.

We sat with our own thoughts for several minutes before Walker finally spoke. "Do you believe in ghosts, Paul?"

Paul, seeming somewhat surprised by the noise, turned his head and looked at Walker. "I don't know. I've never really thought about it. Do you?"

"Oh boy, here we go," I said, shaking my head.

Brook began laughing, probably more than one would expect. Walker started laughing too.

"What's so funny?" Paul finally said, now joining them with several cackles of his own.

"Y'all bunch of pot heads. Get on with it, Walk!" I said, finding myself infected by their directionless humor.

"What? Oh, right," Walker continued. "I believe in whispering winds."

"Whispering winds?" Confusion now painted Paul's face.

"Yeah." Walker continued staring into the distance. The conversation was now likely moving too fast for him. He was in an introspective trance, not knowing who spoke last, wondering if it was his voice or someone else's. I could tell he was trying to figure out whose turn it was to speak.

"Walker ... *my God*, he doesn't know what that means. You are going to have to elaborate!" I was trying my best to help him. I looked at Paul and raised my eyebrows, trying to make fun of Walker, but quickly realized Paul was moving in slow motion as well. Brook was a statue. I was the only one still up to speed, since I refused to join them on their spiritual journey.

Walker turned his head toward Paul and responded, feigning a serious face and pointing at no one in particular. "Whispering winds. They aren't ghosts, in a true sense— more like spirits. You hear them in the breeze, you feel them in the bark of a pine, you see them in that sunset." He now moved his finger in the direction of the fading light. "They call to you. Everyone hears them in their own way, though most never listen or recognize them."

"Where do they call you?" Paul asked, now keenly interested.

"Out there, of course"

"So, they are friendly then?"

"Oh no, not always. It depends on your soul," Walker now looked back out over the town. "Good souls follow the voices and find life out there. A bad soul festers and rots in the wild."

An eerie silence once again fell upon the water tower, oppressing all of us as we tried to consider the meaning of Walker's words, also knowing they were likely a bunch of nonsense.

"Man, this must be some good pot," Paul finally said.

Brook, who all of us including herself forgot was there, laughed and added, "Walker, stop trying to scare us. Sorry, Paul, he has quite the imagination." She glared at Walker and firmly pinched his arm, causing him to jolt.

"Ouch, what was that for?" He yelled.

"What a summer," I said, changing the subject.

"They won't be the same after next year. I don't want to grow up." Brook frowned.

"Are you all going to stay up in Brevard after school?" Paul asked after a moment of reflection.

"Yeah, I think I'll probably stick around after graduation ... I might try to find a job on a farm somewhere," Walker responded sarcastically.

"You know I wasn't talking about you, airhead."

"Well truth be told, with the way dairy farms are going I may be looking for another job next year anyway." Walker feigned a laugh, but we all knew there was nothing humorous about what he had said. As a trickle-down from the Midwest farm crisis of the eighties, many small dairies in Appalachia had gone under. Interest rates were as high as anyone could remember, and land prices had tanked. Davis Milk, with around seventy cows in the milk barn, was struggling to compete with the large-scale productions that were starting to dominate the dairy market. They could operate on small margins with the advantage of high volume, a model unsustainable for family farms. Moreover, Grady was under water after taking out numerous loans to purchase equipment and replace the pumps.

"Don't talk like that, Walk. Grady always figures something out," Brook said as she grabbed his hand.

"Dad's getting old. The farm is more my responsibility every minute."

"Well, to answer your question, Paul, though you should already know, I will be with the 'airhead,' wherever that may be." Brook looked from Paul to Walker and sighed.

"And you?" Paul continued, now directing his question at me.

"Oh, I don't know ... I can't really imagine leaving, but I think I would regret it if I didn't try. I may spend a couple years in the low country and see if I can stomach it. I don't even know what I want to do for work."

"Come back to Charleston with me," he said. "There are all sorts of good jobs down there. It would be easier than finding one here."

"We'll see," I responded. "That's not the worst idea I've ever heard."

"You're not leaving, Chris." Brook smacked Paul on his arm. "Besides, we still have a year until then. Anything could happen."

As time would tell, I never ended up going with Paul to Charleston; Paul himself never went back to Charleston. Brook couldn't have comprehended the truth of her words. Anything could happen, and everything did.

Chapter Eight

SEPTEMBER 5, 1984

MY HEART LENT an aiding hand to my liver this morning as the hangover I surely should have been feeling was thwarted by youthful, eager longing. I hadn't slept more than three hours, and that took place in an empty calf hutch. The previous night was spent at Davis Milk. Walker had invited me, Brook, Paul, and Maddy over for a "couple of drinks." As often happens with friends, two drinks turned into a case and a half of beer and a polished-off bottle of whiskey. At the end of the night— three in the morning—Walker and Brook, inspired by alcohol, hatched a genius plan.

As the girls were getting ready to leave, dizzy-eyed and giggly, Walker asked me if I wanted to go fishing with him the next morning. Surprised by the question, knowing how difficult it would be to wake up early, I responded, "After drinking like this?"

"Mama didn't raise no bitch," was his reply.

"Your dad raised you."

"You want to go or not?" He smiled at me, knowing I wouldn't be able to resist.

"All right, all right. Let's go fish tomorrow. Lonesome Valley?"

Walker nodded as I noticed Brook whispering something into Maddy's ear, causing her to blush and start nodding.

"Eh-hem!" Brook said in our direction. "Maddy has something she would like to ask."

"Do you think, maybe, I could go with you guys? I've been really wanting to learn how to fly fish."

"Of course, you can come!" Walker said, beaming.

"Yay!" Maddy squealed as Brook grabbed her by the shoulders and rocked her back and forth in excitement.

"Okay, so what time should we meet at the trailhead?" I asked.

"Let's try to get there when the sun is still off the fish at the waterfall," Walker responded. "Maybe eight in the mor—shit!" He smacked his knee firmly and looked at me with a frown.

"What? What is it?"

"I forgot I told my dad I'd help him move cows tomorrow at ten. I can't go fishing. I wouldn't be back in time." The tone of his voice sounded kind of funny to me, but I attributed it to being drunk. Then he said, "But Maddy ... you can still go with Chris! Y'all should still go. Chris is better than me anyway, nowadays. At least, he is better at explaining everything. It's just muscle memory to me now."

I now began to get the sneaking suspicion I was being played. *That moron just set me up.*

"Okay," Maddy eagerly responded, turning her gaze toward me. "That is, if you would still want to take me?"

Brook, who stood behind Maddy, was also looking at me, grinning in victory. As if to say Walker was not alone in planning this, she winked at me.

"Let's do it."

Paul, who was probably the drunkest of all of us, stumbled back into the dusty calf barn after walking outside to urinate.

"Everything come out okay?" Walker asked him.

"I don't know, man. Next time you can come with me to help," Paul shot back quickly.

"It would be my pleasure."

"Will you assholes quit with the bickering," Brook said from across the barn. "I swear, every day it seems like you come up with new ways to pick on each other." She looked back and forth from Paul to Walker and then to me before turning back around to pet one of the younger calves. "Can I *please* feed this one, Walk?"

"Fine. He already ate, but you can try offering him another bottle."

Brook walked to the large sink and began thawing out a colostrum bottle from the freezer in a bucket of warm water.

"So, what is that again?" Paul asked.

"Colostrum is the first milk a cow produces after she calves," Walker explained. "It's basically full of nutrients and antibodies they need to get a good jump start in life. Since we have more fresh cows than calves here, we freeze the first few milkings from all the moms and save it to give to the calves we keep."

"If it's so good for them, why does it smell so bad sometimes?"

I laughed. "No, Paul, the colostrum in the other freezer went bad. The power went out, and it sat in the heat for several days. That's why we had to throw it all away." My stomach turned as I reminisced on pouring the chunky, spoiled milk down the drain the previous week.

"Oh, I see." Paul walked over to where Brook was standing by the sink. "Can I help feed him?"

"Sure!" she said, smiling.

Once the colostrum had thawed, they walked over to the small pen that held an eager, hungry calf. "Here, watch me do it," Brook said as she inverted the bottle and helped the calf find the red rubber nipple.

Paul then did something both brave and rash. He reached down and cupped his hands around Brook's, gently holding the bottle. She looked at him with a surprised and somewhat awkward expression. He smiled at her and stopped paying any attention to the calf, putting all his energy into maintaining excessively intimate eye contact with her.

Alarmed, I tried to distract Walker by asking him a question about fly selection the next morning. Unfortunately, he didn't hear me and had already noticed the unprompted move on his girlfriend by Paul.

"Hey man, what are you doing?" he said loudly as he stood up and walked over to the pen.

"Oh, she is just showing me how to feed."

"Well, I think that's enough teaching for tonight!" He grabbed the bottle out of both of their hands.

Brook shyly looked at the floor, obviously embarrassed. "It's okay, Walk, I don't think he meant anything by—"

"It's getting late. Paul, I think you might should head on home. Chris, where are you sleeping?" Walker asked.

At some point while all this was happening, I had laid back against a pile of hay and began noticing how comfortable I was. "I mean, do you think I could just sleep here?"

"Suit yourself," Walker said, rolling his eyes.

"How many times do I twist it before sending it back through? Three?" Maddy asked from across the riffle the next morning, as she struggled to tie her first fly onto the end of the flimsy, translucent tippet that was dancing in the light breeze. She was too focused on her task to see me staring at her, marveling at my morning company. Here I was, ankle deep in a trout stream, paces away from the girl of my dreams. Maddy Caldwell.

My answer was delayed long enough for her to finally look up at me after throwing her hands down to her sides and letting the rod fall to the ground. "Chris! Ugh. Can you help me?"

I began to laugh, causing Maddy to blush. "Okay, okay I'm sorry!" I walked quickly across the stream and took the fly from her. "Let me see what you have going on here, ya dingus. Oh, I see the problem. You have a wind knot at the end of your tippet. That's why the line isn't feeding through the eye right."

"Well, we haven't even started fishing. Do you mean to tell me you sabotaged me?" She smiled and looked up at me. "Or let me guess, Walker used this rod last."

"No, no, it was me." It was my turn to blush.

After snipping off the final three inches of the thin line, I handed it back to her. "Won't you just tie it on for me?" she asked in an overly sweet voice.

"Do you want to learn how to fly fish or not?" An hour later, after untangling Maddy's line from every rhododendron branch in our immediate vicinity, I started to wonder if I had made a mistake. *This creek is too small for a beginner. We should have gone to the Davidson.* Just when I thought our lesson would end in failure, Maddy produced her best cast of the morning. Her false cast created a beautiful visible loop, and her forward cast was timed right as the loop had loaded with tension. The small Adam's mayfly imitation shot forward with perfect speed, fast enough to reach the riffle, but not so fast to splash the surface of the water. It landed daintily at the very beginning of the foam line, right where trout wait for insects to float down the stream.

"Mend! Mend!" I urged her, performing the motion with my own invisible rod.

"I know, I am!" she whispered back.

We both waited in anticipation, leaning forward intensely watching the little fly. *Take it. Take it. Take it.* It lazily floated down toward the end of the current seam almost out of the strike zone. As I was about to curse all the trout in the North Carolina mountains, a small splash submerged Maddy's fly.

"Hit it! Hit it!" I shouted as I jumped for joy. She set the hook immediately and soon had a bent rod tip and a fish on the line. After Maddy stripped in line like I had shown her, I gently netted her first brook trout.

"Chris, it's so beautiful. I've seen pictures, but that doesn't compare to seeing one in person." She was right, of course. Brook trout are the prettiest animal in God's kingdom. This one was no exception. The dark, meandering lines along its dorsum looked like topographic lines on a trail map. Its belly was the color of freshly picked spring strawberries. Along its side, pinpoints of blood red inlaid on sky-blue halos. The remainder of its body was green like the forest around us. The only thing that would steal my eyes from Maddy was a small brook trout and all its vibrancy.

As she had warned me on the drive up the mountain, Maddy refused to unhook her own fish. Despite me explaining that brook trout don't have teeth big enough to cause any real harm, she was terrified she might be bitten, and she didn't want to touch the "pointy end of the hook."

"Let me see it," I laughed as she cautiously handed me the squirmy little trout. With a quick flip of the wrist, the hook was out, and I handed it back to Maddy to release on her own.

"What's it doing?" Maddy asked, flinching, as she extended her arms to hold the fish out over the creek.

"What do you mean? It's not doing—oh," I laughed, "it appears to be laying eggs!"

Maddy screamed as small, squishy orange eggs dripped out of the trout and onto the surface of the stream, softly pulled away from us by the eternal current of mountain water.

"It's fine, just put her back in the water." No sooner than I spoke did Maddy fling the fish back toward the riffle and aggressively wipe her hands on her shorts, leaving slimy streaks behind. She gathered her composure, reeled in all her line, and started dismantling her four-piece rod.

"What are you doing?" I asked, shocked she didn't want to immediately cast back out to the same spot.

"C'mon Chris, can we please go swim now? We've been fishing all morning!"

"All right, all right. Let's go swimming." I copied her and broke my rod down next. Within minutes, our fishing gear was stowed away on the bank next to the waterfall, and we were down to our swimsuits.

"I feel like it's colder now that we have to jump in!" Maddy said, squirming as she stepped out into the shallow tail out. Though I didn't want to admit it, I was very much dreading jumping into the icy water. It had been Maddy's idea to wear swimsuits.

"Oh, it's not that bad," I started to say through clenched teeth as I inched out next to her in the shimmering blue pool. "Okay, I'll go first, but you have to come right be—" Before the sentence had fully fled my mouth, my right foot lost grip on an especially slippery flat river stone. My right leg shot forward, which caused my left leg to slide backward. When I realized I was about to force my body to perform a split—something my ligaments were incapable of—I let gravity pull me down sideways. Though I used my left elbow to brace my fall and surely knocked it on the rocks, the overwhelming sensation I felt as I splashed down into the inches-deep water was cold, bitter and unwelcoming.

When I regained my shocked senses, I realized Maddy was laughing so hard she was snorting and having trouble catching her breath. "It's your turn now!" I shouted as I stood up and started running toward her.

"No! Chris, don't you dare!" She began running back toward the bank but was outmatched by my speed. I caught up to her quickly and swept her off her feet, where she faux struggled in my arms. This is the first time I ever touched her so intimately. Her warm skin, kissed by the summer sun, was smooth against the skin of my chest. The angle from which I held her gave me an impeccable view of her perfectly proportioned body. She screamed as I walked deeper into the pool, and the water from my ankles splashed up on her back.

"Chris, I swear to God, don't, don't, *don't*!"

I loaded by swinging back toward the bank and then tossed her out into the deeper section of the pool, almost close enough to the waterfall to feel mist rolling from the cloud of vapor that hung in the air. Once she hit the water and partially submerged, I—forgoing the cold for the warmth of chasing a beautiful woman—jumped in after her and grabbed her arm. She used her other hand to grab my free arm. We were in a full embrace when she resurfaced. She leaned in as soon as her head came out of the water, before I had time to react, and pressed her lips firmly on mine. I kissed her back passionately, an action eagerly anticipated for many months. After about a minute, we separated and looked at each other sheepishly, hair drenched and disheveled and faces a shade of pale pink from jumping into frigid mountain water.

"Well, that was kind of fun," she whispered.

I smiled at her and felt my face blushing. "Maddy Caldwell, I've been wanting to do that for a while."

"Then why didn't you?"

"You're scary!" I responded, in an exaggerated tone.

She laughed and hit me on the arm. "I'm not *scary*, you're just *scared*."

"Oh, whatever. I did it now. Are you happy?"

"Very." She grinned and kissed me on my cheek.

After our kiss, we swam to the back of the waterfall to the hidden bench that was formed by a rock ledge just below the water's surface behind the falling water. We sat there for the rest of the afternoon while the sun slowly descended toward its resting place on the far side of the horizon.

The little shadows that hovered around the base of the tall trees in the middle of the day were starting to grow at an accelerating pace until they stretched all the way across the pool. The bright, clear air that we fished in was now starting to be replaced by droves of tiny insects shifting and turning between the rays of afternoon light. Everything around us, from the rocks to the trees to the moss growing along the river's edge, started taking on a subtle warm, orange glow. The air itself seemed thicker and hazy as the deep sections of woods around us began losing their source of light, the dense canopy choking out the last gifts of the sun. After talking about everything that came to mind for five straight hours, barely pausing to breathe, Maddy and I decided it was a good time to end our first date.

She stepped out of my Bronco in her parents' driveway at about nine in the evening. Instead of heading toward the porch, she skipped around the front of the truck and opened the driver's side door for one last kiss.

Chapter Nine

OCTOBER 19, 1984

ORANGE AND BROWN leaves, caught up in a shivery autumn gust, swirled around the stoplight and into the empty intersection as Walker, Paul, and I, along with our dates, continued toward the sound of music. The sun had continued its journey west, leaving the mountains illuminated only by the rising moon and the ambient light of the town. As we descended the hill toward campus, we approached the corner toy store, which had a wide display window.

"There's a sight," I said when we were even with the store. Everyone stopped walking and turned to admire our reflection, which was strengthened by the streetlights and contrasting darkness of the store.

Walker's brown hair was slicked back with gel, a rare deviation from his typical unkempt style. His, or rather Grady's, suit hung loosely around his shoulders but fit well elsewhere. Next to him stood Brook, beautiful as ever, wearing a short, skin-tight black dress with full sleeves. Brook's nature of always feeling cold was being masked by liquor and the desire to flaunt her femininity. I never had the slightest desire for that girl but vividly remember the sexual energy radiating from her body that night.

I was the third reflection in line and wore a well-fitting navy suit with a brown tie. My hair was neatly combed but paled in comparison to Walker's masterpiece. My arm was currently clutched by my date for the night, Maddy, whose shoulder-length blonde hair cascaded down over the soft skin of her neck. Her dress was light blue with pink flowers. Like Brook's it had long sleeves but left more to the imagination both in length and fit. She looked elegant and graceful. Her arm, though fully resting on mine, felt as light as air and was warm to the touch. The flickering butterflies of unbridled affection had been taking a toll on my belly the entire walk through town.

The last couple in the vivid October reflection was Paul and his date, Isabelle, a fellow classmate and mutual friend. Paul, in true form, outdressed us all, including the girls. He flaunted a midnight-black tuxedo with a notched, satin-trimmed lapel, silver palmetto tree cufflinks, a coral bow tie, and shiny black loafers. Some tailor on Broad Street in Charleston enjoyed more than one fine meal with Paul's parents' money. Isabelle, who walked away from the reflection to rip a cigarette, was adorned with a mahogany dress.

"I don't know why we had to stop here." Walker's voice ended the silence. "We could have seen our reflection in Paul's shoes."

"I bet if you look close enough, Walker, you'd probably see a real jackass," Paul said, pointing at his shoes. "Go ahead, look!"

"Okay boys, drop your pants. Let me get out my ruler," Maddy interrupted as she pretended to reach into her purse. "Is that what you want?"

"Hope you brought your yardstick," Walker responded, drawing a chuckle from me.

"If she did, I'd beat you on the head with it." Brook proceeded to smack Walker's temple with the back of her hand. "Can we hurry up? I want to dance!" She started skipping down the street, beckoning all of us to follow her.

The Fall Formal was the biggest extracurricular event of the year at Brevard and generally marked the transition from the sweltering days of late summer to the refreshing cool of autumn. The dance was always held in the main courtyard, surrounded on three sides by the administrative office and two academic buildings. The large canvas tent, on standby in case of an evening shower, was not needed that night. The ceiling over the dance floor was simply the heavens with unobstructed constellations and an orange October moon.

"A cup of ice for me and a soda for the lady, please," Walker shouted to the bartender, barely making himself audible over John Cougar's "Jack and Diane." No alcohol was being served that night, since it was an official school event, however Walker had sneaked in a bottle of whiskey. The bartender, likely knowing what was going in Walker's "cup of ice" and Brook's "soda," didn't seem to be bothered by his requests.

Properly liquored, after a few minutes of sipping the burning liquid from Walker's bottle, we all made our way to the dance floor and joined the shifting conglomerate of hopeful romantics. The four of us who had been at Brevard since our freshman year were obviously the most acquainted with the student body and proceeded to explore the crowd for familiar faces. Paul, wealthy and attractive, had no trouble making friends over the last few months and was now dancing with a group of flirting girls, including Isabelle.

Walker, though never a student at Brevard, seemed to know everyone who lived in town and thus knew almost everyone on the dance floor. He may not have liked talking to anyone but me, Brook, and Paul, but everyone at Brevard liked talking to him. He seemed to embody the essence of a small mountain town. He helped run a struggling dairy farm, he was still in love with his junior high school sweetheart, he fly-fished almost every day, and he spent more time in the woods than he did around people. Guys wanted to be him, and girls wanted to be with him. Of course, he never cared about any of that.

"Walker Smokes Davis, get over here, you little bastard!" shouted a beaming classmate of mine, Tom, who was hurrying past people to get to my best friend. "Smokes" was a nickname given to Walker by some of the kids in school. It's still a debate as to whether it was in reference to the Smoky Mountains or attributed to the fact that more than one of my classmates bought a certain medicinal flower from him.

Similar interactions continued for several drinks as "Smokes" was bombarded by my other friends, some exchanging money for small plastic bags full of weed. Finally reunited with our dates, Walker, Brook, Maddy, and I were gently pulled by music to the center of the dance floor. I put the rest of the world in my peripheral vision and focused solely, for the first time, on Maddy.

Now, with her hands gently resting around my neck, I led her in a slow and tender dance that would imprint forever on both of our hearts. Our bodies moved as one to the rhythm of "Time After Time" as we explored deeper the depths of each other's eyes. We continued in small circles around the floor until the song ended, at which point we both leaned in and joined at the lips. The smell of wine and perfume danced around my face and filled my nose as my hands rose from Maddy's waist to the back of her neck.

A firm slap on my backside caused my eyes to sharply pop open in surprise. Assuming the gesture came from my date, I was both surprised and relieved to see Walker standing next to us.

"Attaboy, Chris!" he shouted, as a blushing Maddy and I separated from each other. "Looks like you need a refill. Come on, brother."

Still in a romantic daze, I managed to successfully place one foot in front of the other until Walker and I reached the bar. Instead of waiting in line, we leaned our backs against the counter and watched the crowd. Much to the envy of several onlooking girls, Paul was doing his best to teach Isabelle how to shag, a variation of the swing dance that is popular in South Carolina. Brook had danced her way through the crowd to Maddy, and they were entertaining each other while they awaited our return.

"I actually like Paul," Walker said, turning to me as if for affirmation.

"Yeah, he's a good guy. I mean, he's no Smokes Davis, but I like him too. He brings a little sophistication to our misfit crew."

Walker rolled his eyes. "I'm glad he's the prize tonight. Breaking hearts is exhausting."

I smiled at him. Walker had little vanity, and I knew he was genuinely relieved not to be entertaining the local ladies all night. Something caught Walker's attention in the direction of our dates, causing him to take a step forward from the bar and stretch his neck. My eyes followed his until they found the source of concern. An auburn-haired brute named Jake had pushed through the crowd toward Maddy and Brook.

Jake was one of the few classmates of mine that neither I nor Walker respected. He was highly regarded by himself alone and acted with indifferent, ungrounded confidence. The free-flowing liquor was apparently bolstering his tendencies, and he was making a move on Maddy. Maddy clearly was uninterested and pushed him away several times. Brook's arms were crossed, and her face was stamped with ire. Her mouth was moving, but we couldn't make out her words, due to the distance separating us from the girls. Walker had noticed it first and apparently had seen enough. Once I realized what was happening, I quickly followed him toward the scene.

"Get your hands off of her, asshole!" Brook was shouting as we approached.

"I'm just asking for a dance. Either one of you should feel lucky to dance with me," Jake responded.

"Is that a fact?" Walker now said, walking up to Jake with purpose. "What about me, Jake? Should I feel lucky to dance with you?"

I took Maddy by the arm and pulled her toward me and away from Jake. She looked at me with scared eyes that were only moments before carefree and filled with joy. A burning rage was setting on my heart, and my stomach started churning. I was doing my best to suppress the adrenaline pumping through my arms. Walker's adrenaline was unbridled.

"This has nothing to do with you, Walker. Go back to the farm." Jake shoved Walker on the chest. Words likely wouldn't have pushed Walker past the tipping point, but physical contact was unforgiveable. Unfortunately for Jake, the farm he just mocked had gifted Walker with unsuspected strength and unrelenting toughness. In an instant as brief as flipping a light switch, Walker threw his entire body behind a right hook that caught a dumbfounded Jake on his left cheek. Jake's knees buckled, and he collapsed like a sack of grain onto the dance floor, unconscious.

"Well, that probably does it for this dance," Walker said, quickly looking around. He grabbed Brook and walked off the dance floor in the direction of one of the academic buildings. Maddy looked at me with wide eyes. I grabbed her arm, and we followed our friends into the dark October night.

Although we were only paces behind them, Walker and Brook seemed to vanish into thin air. I assumed they had left campus to avoid any trouble likely to follow the incident on the dance floor. As it would turn out, no one ever confessed who punched Jake. Walker was an idol, and Jake was an unlikeable bully. More than one of our peers would have liked to land a fist on Jake; Walker was the only one rash enough to do it.

Now fully alone, Maddy and I once again turned our attention toward each other. "I'm sorry I wasn't the one to hit him," I told her, looking at the ground. "It should have been me."

"I'm glad it wasn't you, Chris. He got what he deserved, but I don't want to date someone who fights." She hugged me and looked up, drawing my eyes to hers. The fear was once again replaced by romantic longing. Her eyes, barely visible in the darkness, prodded and pulled until I finally surrendered, returning the same unspoken raw emotions she so freely gave me. We remained in a soft embrace for several minutes, saying nothing.

"Well, maybe we should go find somewhere quiet?" she whispered in my ear, grabbing and squeezing my hands.

"Let's," I responded quietly, turning and pulling her by the hand toward the nearest building. When we got to the door, we noticed it was not closed all the way. Excited by the apparent janitorial oversight, I opened the door and beckoned Maddy inside, glancing in both directions of the courtyard before I quietly closed it behind us. The sounds of music and laughter became muted, and I felt my eager heart beating against my ribs.

A short, quiet walk down the main hallway came to an end when we turned into a dark, empty classroom. Ever anxious, I turned again to check the hallway for any signs of life. Maddy, who apparently was tired of waiting, grabbed me by my shoulders, spun my body around, and started to kiss me. She was merciless, barely giving me pause to breathe. She pulled me backward toward a small couch set against the lone window of the room.

She reached her hands around my neck to loosen my tie while I, at the same time, began unfastening the back of her dress. By the time she had fully removed my shirt, her dress was in a loose pile around her ankles. She jumped into my arms, and we collapsed back onto the couch, breathing as one, skin rubbing on skin. Our bodies pulsed with each other, and we never stopped kissing as we blindly pulled the remainder of our clothes off.

With the orange moon shining down on us through the window, Maddy and I surrendered our innocence to each other. My mind has often tried to relive that night, each time no more rewarding than the time before. Although I can conjure the emotions and induce butterflies, I can never remember details. In fact, I don't even remember the color of the couch. It was the first time I had made love to someone, and I am forever grateful it was Maddy Caldwell.

After an unknown period of time spent laughing and talking in tender embrace, now dressed and composed, Maddy and I quietly walked from the classroom into the hallway, hand in hand. Our eyes were now better adjusted to the darkness of the building, and I again surveyed the hallway for any movement or sound.

"Did you hear that?" Maddy asked, as we both became acutely aware of footsteps around the corner to our right. The author of the footsteps must have heard Maddy. All was quiet again, and we seemed to be locked in a standoff. Several minutes passed in silence. I was envisioning scenarios of being expelled for trespassing when I heard an indistinct whisper from around the corner. It was answered by another whisper, softer and feminine. Finally, a head peered from around the corner. Though the previously slicked-back hair was somewhat disheveled, I recognized the silhouette immediately.

"Walker, I should shoot you, you son of a bitch! Y'all scared us half to death." I ran out into the hallway and tackled my best friend, who proceeded to lie on the floor laughing.

"Well, what have you guys been up to?" he finally asked with a grin, looking back and forth from me to Maddy, who was relieved but blushing. Brook now came out from around the corner and greeted Maddy with a smile.

"We could ask you two the same thing," I responded.

"I've never been one to kiss and tell." Walker gathered himself and got back to his feet.

"Well, just in case you decide to start now, I think Maddy and I will go get some air." Brook grabbed Maddy's hand and pulled her toward the door. As they walked down the hallway, Maddy turned around and winked at me. We waited until the door closed behind them before we started to "tell."

"Quite a night," I said, smiling. We both stood there silently, reflecting on our romantic endeavors.

"I told Brook," Walker finally said quietly. My eyes and mouth opened almost simultaneously, as if competing for width.

"Did you tell her what I think you told her?" I responded, dumbfounded.

"It was more like I alluded to it," Walker drew out the annunciation of *alluded*, as if he was also trying to explain to himself what had happened. "I don't know if I'm madly in love or just drunk, but either way, I alluded to a proposal." Walker looked at me confidently, eye to eye, without blinking or looking away. No sheepish grins or blushes.

"Well, it sounds like you ought to get a ring then."

For the first time in either of our lives, we both knew that Walker knew, and now what Brook had always dreamed of seemed to be coming to fruition.

Chapter Ten

NOVEMBER 17, 1984

A PUNGENT BUT familiar smell filled the stand that morning, as Paul looked back down his scope across the field. After a few seconds, he gently shook his head.

As I recollect this memory now, I realize it's been over a decade since I quit dipping tobacco. My lovely wife told me one morning she'd divorce me if I ever got mouth cancer, so that was that. I still remember the empty, unfillable pit in my stomach and the dull aching of my jaw that persisted for the first few weeks as my body shed its reliance on nicotine. With mental toughness and threats from my loved ones, I have been able to resist the ever-present urge. Not a day goes by that I don't deeply crave that calming buzz and empowering mental clarity.

Although I dipped for most of my young-adult life, my mental association with tobacco is now specific to those years in Brevard, the final good years. The scent of dip or even of wintergreen-flavored bubble gum whisks my brain away to the meandering trails, the plunging waterfalls, and the whispering winds of Southern Appalachia. Such was the aroma of the deer stand occupied by me and Paul that cold November day.

"Maybe we were preemptive in our Thanksgiving offer," he said.

"Nah, there's still time. Just be patient."

"I should have shot that buck," he responded.

"And serve everyone musky buck?"

"Yeah, yeah, you're right." Paul looked back down his scope, "C'mon, doe. Come on out from wherever you're hiding. I know you're hungry."

"I know I'm hungry," I mumbled. The sun had only been up for a few minutes, but my stomach was starting to growl.

"Well, we can go to the diner after we're done hunting. A warm cup of coffee and an apple dumpling sound pretty nice right about now."

"No kidding ..." I said almost a minute later, after fantasizing about a mouth full of soft, flaking bread with a sweet, silky apple center, washed down with a sip of freshly roasted coffee.

We both sat back against the wall of the tree stand as we took a break from one sense to focus on another. I'd already killed a deer that season, so I let Paul take lead on this trip. He sat across from me with the butt of the Browning rested on the ground and the stock against the inside of his knee.

I had grown to really like Paul over the previous few months, so much so that I considered him my friend. That may not be a big deal for someone with a lot of friends, but I only had two others. Despite our friendship, however, sometimes when I looked at Paul, I felt resentment toward him. At the time, I didn't understand why I felt that way, and I harbored guilt about it, but I've come to realize it was downright deep-seated jealousy.

Paul seemed to walk through life with ease. He never needed to study for classes, yet he still had better marks than both me and Brook. I don't think he'd ever experienced a pretty girl ignore his ceaseless flirtations. He had picked up fly fishing faster even than I had. But the worst jealousy I felt toward Paul was the quickness with which he and Walker had become such good friends. Why had it been so easy? Would he replace me as Walk's best friend? Am I too old to get jealous over "best-friendship"? These were the questions that clawed at my subconscious when I looked at Paul.

For some reason, those thoughts weighed heavy on my mind that morning as we sat opposite each other in the silent deer stand. Although I should clarify—*we* were silent; the forest was not. In the absence of our voices, nature was coming alive. Gently drifting through the air was the sound of a robin sharply announcing the beginning of a new day. A squirrel scuttled about in the dry, decaying leaves a hundred feet behind the stand. Starting as an unnoticeable breath, an autumn breeze lifted through the valley. From a distant flutter, it grew louder and louder as the trees around us began to feel it. It poured cool air into and out of the stand and continued its way up the mountain. As slow as the crescendo, so also was the decrescendo.

"You know what to do, right? You've actually shot a deer before?" I asked, realizing it was a fairly important question, one that should probably have been asked prior to sitting in the stand.

"Of course, I've shot a deer," he replied defensively.

"Just one?" I pressed.

"Well, yeah." His lips tightened.

"When might that have been?"

"Last year at my uncle's hunting cabin in Georgia."

"All right, well as long as you pulled the trigger."

Fifteen more minutes came and went with no sign of our doe. "How are you and Isabelle?" I asked.

"Oh, I dumped her. I don't know, she just got kind of boring. All she talked about was wanting to go to Charleston and how much money my family had. I got the impression she didn't actually care about me, ya know?"

"Yeah, I know Isabelle. You know, if you actually asked us about girls before trying to make out with them, we could steer you clear of the crazy ones."

"Where's the fun in that?" he asked with a smile.

"Jesus, your high school must have been lame. The rest of us overdosed on flings long ago."

"Can I ask you a question?" Paul murmured, almost inaudibly. I looked up at him. I've learned through the years when someone asks you if they can ask a question, it's usually loaded. Regardless, I nodded.

"You think Walk and Brook will get married?"

"I don't *think* anything. I know that Walk and Brook will get married. You ever read *The Count of Monte Cristo*?"

"No, what's that got to do with anything?"

"Long story short, the main character, Edmond Dantes, was in love with a beautiful girl named Mercedes. In the beginning of the book—and I won't ruin it— Dantes is poor and can't afford an engagement ring. Instead, he proposes to Mercedes using just a piece of twine as the ring. She immediately says yes."

"So?" he asked blankly. Dumbfounded, I stared at Paul's face looking, hoping for some evidence of recognition. None. He had to be the dumbest child of two doctors I'd ever met.

"Soooo, Walker and Brook are like that."

"He proposed with twine?"

"No, he hasn't proposed. The point is that some people are so in love that money and plans don't matter to them."

"That's a book, Chris," Paul finally replied. "Relationships need structure and plans. Hopeless romanticism isn't real life."

"Maybe to you it's not real, but to Walker it is," I said dryly. "What does it matter anyway? Do you have the hots for Brook?"

Silence is an interesting phenomenon. The absence of sound can be perceived so differently, based on the setting. After a long day of work, silence is peaceful and rejuvenating. When hunting, silence is often anticipatory, as you wait for the report of a rifle or shotgun. Silence can be welcome at a dinner party when a family member takes hostage the rest of the table with a story that has been told every Thanksgiving or Christmas. For all the positive silence brings, it can also be excruciatingly painful. The silence of a stethoscope over a previously beating heart. The silence that fills the void left by a lost spouse. The silence I now experienced, sitting in the deer stand with Paul Wright was the unexpected pause that preceded an unsuspected response to a question the asker thought to be obvious. When I recognized the silence, my gut wrenched, and I looked into Paul's eyes.

"Well, do you?"

"I mean, I don't have the hots for her."

"Then what do you have for her?"

"I just like her, that's all. She's one of my best friends. I would never betray Walk, but if they ended up parting ways permanently, I think I would ask if Walker cared if I saw her."

"Not a chance in hell!" I said loudly, not caring it might spook the deer. "First of all, that'll never happen. They have seen it all at this point. They're practically married besides the ring. Secondly, it doesn't matter who Walker is dating. You can't go dating her after he does. What kind of friend does that? Goddammit, if Walker knew you said that! You might think Walker is your friend, but you haven't been paying attention if you think you can get between him and Brook. He'd kill someone for that. I'm not kidding, Paul."

"All right, all right. Forget it. I was just joking around, that's all. Forget I said anything."

"I'm serious. I saw the way you touched her hands that night in the calf barn. I don't like it, and neither did Walk," I said, looking back over the field.

"Clearly," Paul said shortly.

Looking for a way out of the conversation, I leaned forward against the window of the stand and peered out over the clover field. The small crop shifted fluidly with the breeze, giving the impression the deer stand was a small wooden ship in an ocean of faded green. I started wondering if there was too much wind for deer to be moving. They were probably hunkered down in their beds, waiting for a break.

I sat back again and reached down for my thermos. The stale, lukewarm black coffee partially warmed me as it went down. The mental fog was finally beginning to lift. I thought of the previous night spent with Maddy. We had driven dirt roads in the mountains all night, stopping only when we needed more than words to show our affections. She had occupied the largest piece of my mind ever since the Fall Formal. She made everything seem so easy. I had dated other girls at school, but only briefly. None of them had been like Maddy. I played the night over and over again in my head, thanking God she had felt the same way I did. I couldn't mess this one up.

"There she is." Paul interrupted my thoughts by lifting the rifle and looking down the scope toward the back left edge of the field. Apprehensively stepping into the clearing was a mature doe. She stopped upright and stared in our direction for a full minute before gently lowering her head to eat.

"Wait," I said, motioning Paul to lower the barrel. "She will get closer."

"I don't know, she might leave."

"Trust me."

The doe slowly meandered in our direction, stopping every few steps to eat. Growing more confident with each bite, she paid less and less attention to her surroundings. Finally at a comfortable distance, I looked at Paul and nodded. He took a deep breath and looked down the scope. Just when I expected a shot, Paul's eyebrows rose, and he made a last-minute adjustment of the rifle in his arms.

"What are you doing?" I whispered.

"Hush!"

The shot echoed through the mountains, bouncing off peaks and up toward the sky. I looked out into the field and saw the doe bouncing away unscathed.

"What happened?" I asked. "She was right there. We waited all morning for that doe!"

"Look over there." Paul pointed toward the back edge of the clearing. Lying on the ground at the base of an old hemlock was an impressive ten-point buck, breathing his last.

"Damn it, Paul, we don't need a buck. We can't eat that for Thanksgiving. We already talked about this when we saw the last buck. Now you've ruined the whole fucking hunt. The deer will be scared off the field the rest of the day." I was seething. I abruptly stood up, kicked my small stool over, and climbed out of the stand.

"But look at the size of it. That's the biggest deer of the season." Paul looked surprised I was leaving.

"It doesn't matter. That wasn't the point. We aren't trophy hunting right now. We are trying to feed our friends. I guess you can tell them why their meat tastes like shit. Or we'll just bake a bland, dry turkey like everyone else."

"Why do you have such a stick up your ass, Chris?"

"You, Paul, it's you. You are the stick up my ass. It's all just a big game to you. Do you ever think about your actions, or do you just do whatever you think suits you best in the moment?" I thought of his question about Walker and Brook, which only made me madder.

"You can't leave. I need the four-wheeler to get my deer back!" he yelled to me as I walked in the direction of the trail.

"You take it. I'm walking," I said without turning back around. He said something else as I left the field, but the wind drowned his words. Maybe I was overreacting. Maybe not.

Chapter Eleven

DECEMBER 24, 1984

THE QUIETEST PLACE a soul can find itself is in the mountains during a winter snow. Animals disappear as if they never existed. The wind is stilled by heavy, low clouds. Colors gradually fade into shades of white and gray. The comfort of familiar smells is suppressed by the impenetrable blanket of snow and the stinging cold of each breath through your nose. The absence of sound quickly becomes oppressive to those who have never experienced it. The soul is left alone with raw emotions, raw thoughts, raw reflection.

I believe the whispering winds that Walker used to talk about were just the voices of his own heart and mind. His soul called itself into the woods, where it could find reprieve. Though Walker exuded friendly social confidence, he needed to be by himself to recharge. On the morning of Christmas Eve 1984, I woke up to a sloping world of white. Knowing where I would find my best friend, I walked into the woods.

Taking the same trail by the creek that I had used as a child, I passed through an opening in the trees and walked the gentle incline along our shared property line. The only sign of life that morning was a small trail left by a hungry fox, likely from the night before. It seemed erratic, wrapping around the trunk of a hemlock, darting toward the creek, and winding back and forth over the path. If my eyes were sharpened by a lifetime of living in the woods, like they are now, I would have noticed the smaller tracks that blended with the fox's prints; he had been in pursuit of a mouse.

The clouds were beginning to lift, minute by minute. As I walked, small patches of blue began permeating through the heavy sky. I knew it was about to get much colder. As if on cue, a strong winter breeze pushed through the valley, shaking clumps of snow out of the trees. My teeth chattered, and I pulled the collar of my jacket tighter. I trudged forward, the world crunching under my feet as my weight compressed the freshly fallen snow.

At last, I came to a clearing in the woods and an old wooden gazebo. Sitting in the gazebo, gazing out into the quiet world, was my best friend. Although surely hearing my approach, Walker did not turn his head. He sat there as still and cold as an ice-laden riverside stone.

I walked around to the steps on the far side of structure and up onto the platform. Still, Walker did not turn to acknowledge me. Something was amiss. I sat down next to him and put my arm around his shoulders.

"Talk to me, Walk," I said quietly.

He briefly looked at me, emotionless, before turning back to stare into the white forest.

"I can't help you if you don't say anything," I tried again.

"You can't help me, anyway," he finally responded.

"Well, maybe not, but I can certainly listen."

We sat there in silence for a while, listening to the wind whistle through the trees and howl along the valley floor. When I finally looked at Walker again, his head was resting in his hands, and he was staring at the floor of the gazebo.

"Life isn't fair," he said, as a tear fell and gently landed at his feet. "The dairy, Chris, it's done. It's over."

"What do you mean it's over?"

"We're not making money anymore. We have been eating into Dad's savings every month since July. Milk production is down, our calving rate is garbage, and the cows haven't been putting on weight. Damn it, we should have known months ago."

"Known what?"

"It's Johne's, Chris. The whole fucking herd has Johne's."

My heart stopped, understanding the gravity of what he just told me. Johne's disease is a condition characterized by diarrhea and weight loss, caused by a bacterium closely related to the ones that cause tuberculosis and leprosy in people. It infects most ruminants and has the worst impact on dairy cattle herds. Though often fatal, most of the impact is economic, as the infected cows don't show immediate signs and rather chronically waste away, dropping in milk production and body weight, both things that are important for the dairy business.

"Walk, I'm so sorry," I said quietly. "Is there anything you can do? Can you start replacing them?"

"We have been culling the sick cows, or at least the ones with diarrhea, but we'd have to start from scratch to get rid of it. It's everywhere now, all over the farm. We don't have the money to start over. Our volume has been dropping every month this year. We were already in trouble with milk prices and competing with the big dairies. This is just the nail in the coffin."

"Well, what are you going to do?" I asked.

"If I knew, do you think I'd be sitting here?" he snapped back at me. "What the hell are we supposed to do?"

"I don't know, I'm just trying to—"

"There's something else," Walker said, looking away from me. "The money for Brook's ring is ... gone." He saw the pain in my eyes as he muttered the short but definitive word.

Gone.

"I didn't have a choice. Grady is out of money, so I had to use it to help the farm. This cold world has shattered not only my hopes and dreams, but now it's stolen them from Brook. She doesn't deserve this. She doesn't deserve me."

"She loves you, Walk. She'd go to hell and back for you," I said, trying to encourage him. My words only compounded his heartbreak.

"I know, Chris, but that's the point. I can't let her do that. She needs someone whose life doesn't force her to hell and back. I'm starting to feel like I should let her go." He could barely get the words out over a wavering voice.

"You can't just give up on yourself like that. Brook needs you, and you need her! You will figure something out, even if that means leaving the farm. There is no reason to sink with the ship, Walker. You're not responsible for the financial decisions your father made over the last twenty years. You're young, man. You can find something else to—"

"And give up on my dad?" Walker's face distorted, and his eyes narrowed as he shot the question at me. "Sometimes I forget that you're not from here ... and then you make comments like that. Family is everything. I'm not walking out on Grady, and I don't want to hear you ever say those words again. Family is all I got."

Walker stood up, looked at me with dismay, and turned to walk home.

"I'm just trying to help you, Walk!" I yelled as he left me sitting in the gazebo alone.

"Well, you're not. Stop trying."

I watched as Walker slowly disappeared into the snow-covered forest. A strong gust of wind rattled my bones. I stood up, turned toward our house, and left nature by itself again. I knew there was only one thing I could do to help. I had to talk to Brook.

Hindsight is a gift of the devil. He waits until all else is quiet before gently whispering into your soul, making you believe you could have changed the past, present, and future. My drive to the Palmers' house Christmas Eve of 1984 has lived in the darkest depths of my mind for thirty-four years. Every once in a while, in the stillness of night, restlessness grabs me and brings me in earshot of the evil murmuring, "If you hadn't told her ..."

Brook and her father, the latter already on the bottle, were sitting on the porch, watching the snow fall on their land as I came to a sloshing halt in the Bronco. My eyes rested on Brook as I opened the door and stepped out into the mixed slush of snow and mud. She looked calm, even peaceful, sitting next to her father, admiring the white blanketed landscape. I knew my words were going to break her heart, but it seemed like the only way to save her. She knew Walk better than even I did, and she would know what to say to calm his nerves and restore his hope in his future—in their future.

"Mornin', Chris." Mr. Palmer cut the cold air with his words, which were visible as a white mist. "I figured you would be cutting up with Walker this morning."

"Yeah, I did too," said Brook softly. "You always spend Christmas Eve with Walk. If I knew you weren't with him today, I would have called him."

"I was with him, but I needed to see you," I said, making eye contact with Brook, whose eyes widened to reveal skinny rings of white around the ever-present brown.

"Okay, well let's go inside. I'll put a pot of tea on."

The Palmers' house was simple on the inside and surprisingly clean, despite Brook's mother having walked out on them several years before. Brook took care of Mr. Palmer the best she knew how, and that included most of the cooking and cleaning. Brook led me into the small sitting room, just inside the front door and left me there while she went to the kitchen to make us both some Earl Grey.

Alone with my thoughts, I looked around the room and pondered. A small, framed picture of Walker and Brook at high school homecoming rested on the mantel over the small fireplace. I thought about Brook and her mother. The person most responsible for her well-being and stability abandoned her. This forced Brook to grow up much faster than the rest of us. Brook's father took to the bottle hard after his wife ran away as his coping mechanism, and Brook learned quickly that it was up to her to care for herself and her drunk father every single day, no matter what life dropped at their feet. She felt she owed him that much, at least, since he and not her mother committed to raising her, regardless of how effective that was.

Of course, when drinking, her father was unable to give her the kind of emotional support she needed to continue pouring herself out for them. This is where Walker filled in. Walker lost his mother to disease as a young boy and thus was in the same position as Brook, though without the alcoholic father. Grady, for the most part, was able to care for himself and Walker through the dairy but required Walker's help to keep it profitable. Walker, like Brook, had little emotional support. He would tell you he didn't need that kind of love, but he'd be wrong. No one can traverse the convoluted path of life without someone gently holding together the pieces of their heart. Brook and Walker became that for each other.

That being said, anyone who has been romantically in love knows the danger of resting the weight of your own world on your lover alone. Finally, this is where I came into the picture. I was the third party. Friend to both, but in love with neither, I was content to calm the floodwater of both of their lives, so that they did not drown each other. I was their friend, that was my job.

Looking at the picture on the mantel caused my gut to wrench. Walker's words echoed through my mind. *She needs someone whose life doesn't force her to hell and back. I'm starting to feel like I should let her go.* He couldn't let her go. Brook would gladly walk hand in hand with Walker through all of life's worst valleys if it meant their souls would remain in that eternal embrace. Walker was being unreasonable, and if Brook confronted him about it, he would realize that, surely.

The strong smell of black tea followed Brook into the room as she closed the French doors behind her. She set the mugs down on the coffee table and sat down next to me on the couch.

"Honey?" she asked while stirring a small dollop into the black liquid. I shook my head gently, stomach still churning. "What's going on, Chris? You seem so serious, and it's Christmas Eve. It's simply a rule that you can't be sad on Christmas Eve."

I took a small sip of the warm, bitter tea and looked up at my friend. "It's Walker. He's not doing well, Brook."

"Is it about the farm? He told me about the Johne's."

"They are pretty much out of money. It sounds like the farm may go under, save a miracle," I said.

"Miracles can happen. They have before."

"It's more than that."

"Well, what is it? You're scaring me, Chris."

"He thinks this all is bad for you and—"

"Bad for me?" she interrupted. "What does it have to do with me? It's just the dairy. They will figure it out, and if not, Walker can do something else. I will be making money soon anyway. I don't understand."

"He says you deserve better, Brook. He says he doesn't want to put you through all of this and is wondering if you should even be together anymore."

Brook shook her head from side to side. "He's just being dramatic and silly. He can't mean that. He has a ring! He told me he has a ring. We're going to be engaged, Chris. He can't mean that."

I stared at the ground, saying nothing. The words were in my mouth, but they tasted sour. Tears started to flow over the rim of Brook's eyelids, and I saw one gracefully wet the hardwood plank near my feet.

"He has a ring, right, Chris? Tell me he has a ring!" Her voice was growing frantic with desperation, but I couldn't look at her. "Chris!"

"He had to use the money. There's no ring." The words hurt as they left my mouth.

"No," she whimpered, "he can't mean it. He is just being silly." She sobbed between sentences, and her voice wavered with each word. "He's just being silly." Brook stood up, wiped her eyes, and rushed out of the room. I sat until I heard the engine of her car turn over and the sound of her tires track down the icy gravel driveway. As if waking from a nightmare, I slowly stood and walked to the porch and took a seat in the rocking chair opposite Brook's father.

"Well, she is sure in a tizzy," he slurred as I reached for his bottle of brandy.

"No doubt," I said softly, almost whispering. I threw the bottle back and drank the sweet, burning liquor until the need for another breath caused me to pause, tears trickling down my cheeks all the while, freezing before they could fall from my face.

I waited in silence for what seemed like a lifetime on Brook's front porch with her father. I had no intention of interrupting the conversation they so desperately needed to have. However, I was negligently unaware that I may have done the very thing I was trying to avoid by preemptively talking to Brook. After several hours passed, I left the Palmers' house in the direction of my home and, more importantly, Davis Milk.

The clear skies of mid-morning had been filled with gray afternoon clouds, so heavy and low you could almost reach out and take a piece. As I crossed over the small bridge that spanned the Davidson, snow began falling again. At first it was light and delicate, but the closer I got to home, the more it seemed to pick up. By the time I turned off the highway toward our finger of the valley, it was bordering on a blizzard. It wasn't until I stopped the Bronco in Walker's front yard that I saw Brook's car sitting there. I assumed she would have been gone by then, especially with the deteriorating weather. I decided to wait. I had waited on Brook's porch, and I would continue to wait outside Walker's house until they were finished.

Before the hood of the Bronco had stopped steaming, I saw a light coming from the Davises' house; someone had opened the front door. The first silhouette was Brook's. She stopped and turned around with her hands raised, visibly distraught. She was shouting something. I cracked the door and strained to listen, but the blizzard drowned all sounds but the frozen, howling wind. Walker's silhouette came into frame next, outlined by the warm light of the small farmhouse. He reached for

Brook's hands, but she quickly retracted them. Again, he tried reaching out to her, this time to grab her shoulders, but she shoved him in the chest, sending him reeling backward into the house.

The light of the house disappeared with the slam of the door. Brook turned and ran down the steps, leaning forward with her hands in her coat. She wept as she ran toward her car, seemingly struggling to catch her breath. In an instant, without even noticing me, she left the farm behind. Her taillights faded into the blowing snow, and she was gone.

What have I done?

Chapter Twelve

MARCH 1985

THE WINTER OF 1985 was bitterly cold, in the mountain air and in all our hearts. Brook had desperately tried rekindling Walker's feelings for her several times after the turn of the year, but to no avail. Walker's heart was as solid and emotionless as bedrock. He had convinced himself that he was bad for Brook, and that was that.

Rare breaks from the daily toils at the dairy left Walker desperately searching for the bottom of the bottle—every bottle. Brook's heart was not the only one Walker had broken Christmas Eve 1984. I had lost my best friend, and it felt that life as we knew it had met its bitter end. To make matters worse, time was running short as the spring semester drew to a close.

Several times I walked the old cornfield trail toward the Davises' farm, only to halt paces from its end as fear welled up in my throat. Walker and I had been best friends, almost like brothers, for as long as my memory stretches. However, I knew in my heart he blamed me for everything that happened with Brook. *After all, I'm the one that told her.*

I didn't see much of Walker until the spring began bringing new life to the town and surrounding valley. The rare encounters we did have left me wanting no more. Although the following months would bring true horror, one night in March especially stands out to me and works its way into the folds of my memory even now, so many long, long years later.

It's interestingly grim how nature or God—whatever you want to believe—knows when tribulation is at hand. No sooner does tragedy strike than the clouds well over and shed their tears. The beginning of March was a continuation of February, with snowstorms frequenting our valley. Late March, however, brought weeks of cold, depressing rain, making the rivers practically unfishable. The gin-clear waters of Appalachia were stained with mud and soot. Of course, that didn't matter much for Walker. He was too drunk to fish.

It was raining like the devil most of the day March 23. During the brief pause in the early evening, I left Maddy's house to head home, stopping briefly in town for a glass bottle of Coca-Cola that I would fill with peanuts, my favorite snack.

"Look at this ass," I muttered to myself as I passed a staggering silhouette on the corner of Main Street. I looked at my watch and remarked to myself something witty about the early hour in which this man was entirely inebriated. I parked not far past the silhouette and started walking toward the convenience store. I felt two drops bounce off my hat almost simultaneously as I neared the door. Soon the sky would open again. The air felt heavy.

"Hey, there's Chris, my old pal, my old bud, my old ..." The immediately recognizable voice tapered off, as it had forgotten where it was headed.

Oh God, I thought to myself, *Walk ...*

"Aren't youuu gonna say something to me? Look at me. *Look at me!*"

"I don't want to look at you," I quietly responded as the cold rain began wetting my clothes. "Not like that."

"Like what, Chris? It's your—your fault anyway."

I knew this was coming, and I winced at the accusation. I responded anyway. "I didn't make you drink that alcohol. What the hell are you doing this drunk at seven in the evening? What's wrong with you, Walk? Pull it together, for God sakes. You're better than this."

He stepped in place unnecessarily with his right foot to correct a sudden lapse in balance. His eyes, glazed over, seemed to be focused just past my left ear. "You know what I mean. You put your nose in my fucking business, and nooow look. You and Brook did, did this to me."

"I was trying to help you, Walker, and you're the one that said she—"

"Fuck you, you can't help me. *No one* can help me. You should never have tried, Goddammit!" Walk snarled through clenched teeth. The rain was steady now, even heavy.

"All me and Brook ever did was love you, you piece of shit. You'll see that when you sober up." I had had enough.

"I am sober. I'm sober enough to—" Walker then fell to his knees, wretched and vomited up an inordinate amount of whiskey.

"Yeah, you're sober, all right," I said turning my back on him. "I'll see you some other time, 'Smokes.'"

With equal parts of tears and rain now streaming down my cold, numb face, I walked to the Bronco, forgoing the Coke. When I turned on the lights, the silhouette I had seen when I first pulled up was kneeling on the ground, obviously sobbing in a puddle of his own vomit. "Look at this ass," I muttered to myself once more. Only this time I knew the ass was my best friend, at least he used to be. *I still have Brook and Paul,* I thought to myself as I threw the Bronco into first gear. Little did I know, the next evening would complicate even those relationships.

"Come on, Paul," I said to myself the following night as Brook and I waited in the driveway of the house he—his parents, really—rented that semester.

"Oh, don't be in such a rush. Just enjoy the moment, Chris," Brook said from the passenger seat.

"Easy for you to say. You don't have an exam in two days. At least I'm actually coming," I retorted. Maddy decided to prioritize our exam over a night in Asheville, and thus was not joining us that evening. It was probably better that way. The last thing I wanted was for this to feel like a double date.

"Whatever, since when do you need to study anyway? You are so *smart*!" The way she said it left me wondering if she was truly complimenting me or rather being sarcastic. I was smart back then, though, and really didn't need to study anymore. The same could probably not be said for Paul, who, after starting the previous semester with great grades, had underperformed on the last two exams he had taken. *Some doctor he will make.*

"Look, here he comes now! Get in, Paul. Chris is getting so *grumpy*!" She playfully punched my arm.

The drive to Asheville from Brevard involves driving thirty or so minutes on a straight mountain highway, over several rivers and past forests and cow pastures.

"There's another dairy that went under," Paul said quietly as we passed a dilapidated pasture fence with an empty barn offset in the background.

"Nice, Paul. Way to read the room," I said, looking back at him in disbelief. *Is he trying to make Brook upset?*

Brook didn't respond, but instead asked, "What are you guys getting for dinner? I think I'm going to get some pecan trout with grits!"

My stomach growled in response as I thought about my dinner selection. It had been a while since we drove to Asheville for dinner. The last time we went, Walker had been with us. I shook the thought from my head. "I think I'm going to get some steak and potatoes, something that will stick to the ribs."

"I just can't wait to start drinking. I've been studying for over an hour, and I'm ready to let loose," Paul said from the back seat.

"A whole hour? My goodness, how do you do it?" was my response, making Brook giggle.

It was dark by the time we arrived at the steakhouse. Dinner was fairly uneventful, as we were all more occupied with filling our stomachs than having small talk. Brook and Paul polished off a bottle of pinot noir, and I drank whiskey on the rocks. It was the best dinner we'd had in a while, and we even shared cheesecake for dessert. After we finally rose from the table, Brook said, "Let's walk around downtown. I want to go down by the river." We agreed and walked down Main Street toward the French Broad River, a dirty, brown tailwater that I liked to call Trasheville River, mostly because I had never had luck catching fish out of it.

Paul led us to a rusted iron bench that overlooked a large bend and pulled out a small flask of moonshine.

"More liquor?" I asked, hesitant to continue drinking with the drive ahead of us.

"Why not? Here, have a pull."

"No thanks, I think I'm going to hold off."

"What about you, little girl?" Paul asked Brook. I looked at him curiously. *Little girl?*

"Okay, fine, I'll have a pull." She threw the flask back and coughed a couple of times before returning it to Paul. "Well, this has been a nice evening. Thank you for dragging me away from the house. I love my father, but it is so tiresome telling him things two to three times for him to even remember."

"He probably needs help," I said seriously to Brook. "He has been drinking more and more these days."

"Oh, c'mon, Chris," Paul said from the far side of the bench. "No need to get so serious. Let's just enjoy the moment." He waited several minutes. "Brook, you should come live in Charleston after school. My parents could help you get into nursing school or whatever it is you want to do. They know so many important people down there."

"You really think their word would pull weight?"

"Absolutely. You would thrive down there, with your tan skin and beautiful figure. It's like you were made to live at the beach."

He's going too far.

"Maybe. I do think I would miss it up here. I've always thought I would stay ..." she said, her voice trailing off.

The conversation was going in a direction I didn't like, so I stood up and walked toward the river. I pulled the metal can out of my pocket and grabbed a pinch of moist wintergreen long-cut tobacco. I stuffed it in my lower lip on the right side and felt the sweet burn and resultant buzzing in my head. I began to wish Walker was with us. I loved Brook and tolerated Paul, but I only ever had one true best friend, and he was missing from my life. Before I realized it, my eyes began to water, and I reached up to wipe them. Unfortunately, I forgot I had just used those fingers to pack tobacco. The burn that had been welcome in my mouth now stung my eyes like fire.

"Goddammit," I cursed under my breath as I blinked repeatedly. When the burning finally dissipated, I decided to return to the bench. When I found myself in hearing range of Brook and Paul, I was shocked.

"What are you doing?" I heard Brook ask earnestly.

"Something I should have done a long time ago."

Before I could say anything to stop him, Paul leaned in and kissed Brook firmly, right on her lips. Brook let him linger longer than I would have liked before finally pulling away in confusion.

"Paul, what did I fucking tell you?" I ran over to him and pushed him off the end of the bench.

"Chill out, man. It's just a kiss. Jesus Christ. Isn't she single now? Brook, aren't you single?"

Brook didn't say anything. She seemed to be struggling to process what had just happened and stared at the ground in disbelief.

"That's not the point!" I was livid. It was true that Walker ended his relationship with Brook, but after years and years of being inseparable, it didn't seem right for someone else to kiss her. I felt as though I had watched someone other than my father kiss my mom.

"Let's go home," was all I could say, though I'm sure the redness in my face and the throbbing vein in my neck said much more.

Chapter Thirteen

APRIL 12, 1985

"I COULD LAY up here all day," I said, looking over toward Brook, whose eyes were closed as her head rested against the sloping roof line. Every spring when the sun started warming the shingles, Brook and I would lie on the Palmers' roof and watch life come back to the mountains. When we were younger, Mr. Palmer would drunkenly yell at us, "Climb down from there. You'll f-fall off!" Now that we were older and at least projected a sense of responsible, he ignored us.

"I needed this. It's been months since I've felt any warmth." Brook opened her eyes and looked at me. "Have you talked to Walk?"

"I went by the dairy yesterday morning after the early milking. He's getting better. I think Grady finally said something about his drinking."

"Good."

A yellow swallowtail fluttered effortlessly overhead toward the butterfly bushes by the Palmers' porch. It landed on one of the smaller clusters of leaves and crawled around, looking for nectar. Being too early in the year, none was found, and the dainty butterfly allowed itself to be lifted back into the air by the midmorning breeze.

"What about you? Have you talked to him?" I asked.

Brook frowned and shook her head. "He's still not interested in talking to me. I just don't understand. He has always been stubborn, but it's like he won't give us a chance."

"Yeah, I don't know, Brook. I would like to think he just needs time. I've never known him to give up on anything. You know it's him and not you, right?"

"No, that's a silly thing to say. He's putting words in my mouth. I don't need him making decisions for me. I'm a grown woman, and I have always known what my future looks like with Walker. It seems he is the one that failed to consider it. I love that boy, and I love that farm."

"I know you do." I watched the butterfly float further and further away until it disappeared into the background. "I don't know what to tell you to do at this point."

"We are running out of time, Chris! We graduate next month. I have to make plans for my life, if it's not going to be on that farm. Daddy's talking about moving back to Charleston." That was news to me.

"Wait, you can't be serious." My heart sank. "When?"

"August, probably. And I'll be honest, Chris, I'm going to have to go with him if Walker doesn't ask me to stay."

"But your dad has family and friends down there that can take care of him. You don't have to go just because he goes."

"Yeah, but why would I stay? What is here for me now?"

I would have said *I am*, but the truth is, since Brook and Walker fell apart, I had also stopped planning for my future. It seemed like everything depended on the dynamic of our trio. We were supposed to have plans together.

"I think you should consider moving to Charleston too, Chris." Brook reached out and rested her hand on my shoulder. "Paul said his parents can help me get into nursing school. Their recommendations carry a lot of weight at MUSC. I'm sure they can help you find a job too, at least until you figure out what you want to do."

"I just haven't thought about it yet, and I don't really want to. I'm not ready to give up on Walk."

"What if Walk gives up on you?"

After a moment, I wiped the dampness from my eyes with my sleeve. Deep down, I knew Brook was right. "Regardless, I don't think I would let Walker find out it's Paul's idea that you move to Charleston."

"Frankly, I don't care if he does. I don't owe him anything at this point, and neither does Paul," Brook replied curtly.

"Are you forgetting what happened last month?" I asked, referring to our trip to Asheville with Paul.

"Oh, that again? Boys are boys, Chris. I didn't kiss him back."

"It doesn't matter. He tried to kiss you. Can you imagine if Walker found out?"

"No, I can't, but he doesn't own me. He's made that crystal clear, so what does it matter anyway? Even if I did kiss him back, neither Paul nor I would be doing anything wrong."

"Walk wouldn't see it that way, and you know it." Walker was in a vulnerable, emotional state. I suspected he was not happy Brook was spending time with Paul. Paul had quickly become one of our best friends, but I grew concerned that the situation with Brook had changed all of that.

"Ugh, that silly boy. I can't just wait for him forever. He's got until graduation, but if he doesn't come around,

I'm moving to Charleston with my dad, and you should too."

"I'll think about it."

The cry of an eagle echoed through the valley.

"Can you see him?" Brook asked.

"Not yet," I said as I squinted and searched the horizon. Brook was resting her eyes again. I looked over at her and felt pity. Her face was soft and expressionless. She looked content, but I knew nothing was further from the truth. The spring had taken its toll. Her eyes were constantly framed by heavy bags, and she had clearly lost weight. Her already dainty extremities looked like knobby twigs. The sound of ruffled feathers on the wind drew my attention away from Brook and up into the sky above us.

"There he is!" I exclaimed, causing Brook to sit up. The richly bronze golden eagle started its dive immediately overhead and shot down like a German Stuka into a thicket at the edge of the woods. We watched until the eagle took flight once more with a small field mouse struggling to free itself from the eagle's long, slender talons.

"All right, I guess it's about that time," I said, standing up and turning toward the branch that overhung the roof. "I told Paul I'd meet him to fish midmorning. I'm sure he's there by now."

"I'm glad you're still getting to fish, even if it's not with Walk," Brook said as she also got to her feet.

"Yeah, me too."

After hugging Brook goodbye, I climbed in the Bronco and started making my way toward my favorite place in the world. Brevard seemed quiet that morning, other than a small crowd by the diner. I found my mind pondering Brook's suggestion about moving to Charleston. It's not the first time I'd considered it. Paul had first mentioned it that night on the water tower, and it had been ever present in the background of my consciousness since. It probably was the most reasonable option for my future.

Even if Walker and I could go back to normal, which I fully expected would happen, it still didn't leave me with much to do in Brevard after graduation. My degree was in business management. The only "business" I had worked with in Brevard was the paper mill, and they already had a manager—my father. No other businesses in town seemed to need a new manager, as most were family owned and operated. Charleston, on the other hand, had no shortage of business opportunities.

The thought left a bitter taste in my mouth and, as had become pattern, I ignored it and tried to redirect my attention. I rolled the windows down and breathed a deep breath of fresh Appalachian air. *This is home*, I thought to myself. I couldn't imagine returning to the rhythmic chaos of a larger city.

I finally turned onto the gravel road that led to the trailhead. I likely could have driven the rest of the way with my eyes closed. Instead, I reached to the passenger-side floorboard and retrieved my bottle of whiskey. Although I had no interest in drinking, it felt customary to take a long pull. I drank for Walker. He hadn't been fishing with me since before Christmas, but I always felt like he was in the seat next to me. "Soon enough, buddy," I whispered.

When I rounded the final curve of the dusty old forest service road, there were two vehicles at the trailhead. One of them was Paul's Camaro and, to my horror, the other vehicle was one of Grady's old farm trucks—Walker's truck.

"Shit, shit, shit," I said as I hurriedly got out of the Bronco and grabbed my gear. To my knowledge, Walker had not known Paul had kissed Brook or that Paul was convincing Brook to move. The problem was that for all of Paul's redeemable qualities, he was also an arrogant jerk and didn't understand social cues. Frankly, I did not trust him not to brag to Walker about his and Brook's relationship.

Before I realized it, I was sprinting down the trail, hopping over roots and cutting corners through the spring hardwood stands. Despite the temperature being in the low forties, I was sweating when I reached the switchbacks. Instead of walking the full mile, back and forth, slowly making my way down the trail, I decided to sit and slide down the steep mountainside from trail to trail. The first attempt was smooth, and I landed nearly on my feet. The second cut-through was less smooth. My pants caught a prominent exposed root halfway down the hill and swung me around, ripping them in the process. I came sliding down to the next trail face-first, hands extended in front to brace myself.

My hands were roughened and starting to ooze blood when I came to a stop, but I couldn't feel anything more than the panic I was already experiencing. I stood up again and started running down the straight trail, switchbacks behind me. I stopped to catch my breath at the white pine and wiped the sweat from my eyes.

When I finally reached the almost-hidden shortcut to the top of the waterfall, I slowed my pace to a walk. There was no reason to alarm them if everything was fine, and I could already hear Walker giving me hell for making a scene over nothing. I was probably overreacting, but I couldn't shake this sense of dread. It felt like the mountains were telling me to hurry, thrusting me forward.

The shortcut more resembled a game trail than a walking trail. I brushed most of the waxy rhododendron leaves aside as I passed through the riparian forest. They say you should always go hiking with someone taller than you in the lead. I did not have this luxury and was soon spitting spider webs from my mouth. Spring sunshine flooded through the opening at the end of the woods.

The thundering echo of the falls quickly engulfed me as I stepped slowly into the cool water at the head. I kneeled and slowly inched toward the precipice until I came to a stop on an exposed river stone. Sure enough, when I looked over the edge into the crystal-blue pool below, I saw Paul and Walker fishing side by side with no more than thirty feet separating them. I looked upward and sighed in relief. They were just fishing together, nothing more.

Feeling awkward in my current position of espionage, I stalled for a moment as I tried to decide how I was going to join them in the pool. I decided it would be more casual if I joined them from the regular trail rather than the shortcut. As I turned to leave the falls and wander back through the green tunnel, I heard a shout—a heated shout. My heart skipped a beat, and my throat felt heavy. My eyes instinctually closed. I waited for about ten seconds, at which time came the second roar. I must have turned to face the pool again because when I opened my eyes, I saw Walk and Paul. Though this time there were no more than ten feet between them, a number rapidly shrinking.

Neither Paul nor Walker was holding a fly rod. Paul seemed to be in the same spot from which he fished. Walker, however, was closing in on him quickly.

"Don't do it Walk. Don't, don't, don't ..." I pleaded with him quietly, knowing he would not hear me over the sound of the river. I knew I needed to do something. I had to intervene. I tried to stand up, but my knees felt weak and heavy. *C'mon Chris!* I thought. *Get up. Shout! Do something. Do anything!* To this day, I truly believe I was about to stand up. I know in my heart I would have.

Sadly, I did not intervene in time. Walker threw the first blow. An unrestrained right hook caught Paul under his left eye and split his cheek open, spilling sharp, red blood into the untarnished water of our holy fishing place. This was enough to get me moving. I started trying to make my way down the side of the falls. My legs were shaking, and I could barely hold my footing on the wet rocks. I knew I had to get to the bottom before they would see or hear me, since the side was covered by foliage. They were also so concentrated on each other I was worried no amount of shouting would alert them to my presence.

The weight of Walker's first blow sent Paul almost to his knees. He responded with the back of his elbow, as he exploded back to his feet. Now Walker's blood mixed into the river. Walker took the fight to the ground, as he usually did when his opponent was man enough to fight back. He drove his shoulder into Paul's chest, and they both went crashing into the knee-deep water together, shouting and cursing.

What happened next changed our lives forever, changed our town forever, and for so many people, changed the mountains forever. Knowing he was losing the fight from his back, Paul reached for the first thing he could find, a river stone about the size of his fist. Luckily for Walker, the swing missed his head, slamming against his shoulder instead. Walker's eyes turned to fire, and I saw a look from my best friend that I thought him incapable of producing; I saw pure, unbridled hatred. Walker clenched Paul's arm, which was now powerless, and grabbed the stone.

As time stood still and I with it, Walker threw all his weight—all his fury—behind the stone and bludgeoned it into Paul's temple. In a moment as short as a hummingbird's wingbeat, all the life in Paul's body was exhaled into the Appalachian breeze and carried away, never to return.

Gasping for air and choking on my own spit, I reversed my course and started frantically scaling the side of the waterfall back toward the top, toward my escape from this place of terror. My body was numb. No amount of physical pain could break through the shock that was rapidly setting in. I only knew the rocks had cut my hands when I saw my blood trickling down into the edge of the pool. I couldn't stomach the sight of any more blood, and somehow, I didn't want my blood to join theirs in the pool. It was defiled enough.

I looked over my shoulder one last time. The body of Paul Anderson Wright lay motionless in the pool, with Walker squatted over it in disbelief. He looked back and forth from Paul to the stone. The stone fell from his hand, and Walker dropped to his knees and began shaking Paul's body by the shoulders. He started shouting, shaking the lifeless body progressively harder. When Walker's mind at last whispered to him the truth, Walk laid his head down upon Paul's chest and sobbed. My ears began to ring. I needed to get off the rock face.

I finally pulled myself over the edge and crawled, heaving, to a spot near the bank. The sand under my hands started to darken with red, causing the ringing to get louder. My abdomen violently constricted, and vomit poured from my mouth. The world around me started to spin and get dark. I was not yet out of the stream. Helplessly I started to collapse toward the water. *I ... will drown*, a voice in my head told me as I neared the river. My body would not respond. *This is it.*

"Here, take my hand," a kind voice in front of me said.

I know that voice.

As if in a dream, I raised my head and looked up to take the extended hand. Kneeling on the bank, dressed as he was when I first met him in Brook's driveway, and smiling a big Charleston grin, was the image of Paul. I was gently pulled from the water and laid on a patch of riverside moss.

"I'm Paul," he said, voice trailing off as my mind finally surrendered. The world shrank from the peripheries as a deep blackness took hold. The last thing I remember was a thin trail of morning mountain mist slowly rising from the spot Paul stood on the bank, reaching toward the heavens.

I've lived the remainder of my life trying to understand what I saw as I passed out on the riverbank that day. Was it a near-death experience? Was it really Paul stopping to save me as he made his way to the afterlife? Was it God? Maybe it was just a hallucination. Whatever it was, I have been eternally grateful because it saved me from almost-certain death.

Chapter Fourteen

APRIL 13, 1985

IT'S INTERESTING THAT your senses start working before your mind when you first awaken in a strange place. It was dark when I finally came to on the banks of the creek at the head of the falls. In exhausted delirium, my eyes searched the surroundings. Initially I assumed I was home in bed, but the cold April air sharply reminded me I was still in the valley, and moreover reminded me of the horror that preceded my collapse. I wished I could go back to sleep and make the events of the day permanently vanish like the breathy fog rhythmically exiting my mouth and nostrils as I began to comprehend the danger of my current state.

My ears seemed to wake next as they took in the peaceful, yet suddenly eerie sound of water flowing through utter darkness. Coyotes yipped and howled deeper in the valley. The chirping of bats overhead and the lengthy hoot of a nearby owl joined the busy sounds of the living forest. The mountains seemed more alive than they were during the sunlit hours.

I could feel my heart beating against my rib cage, pressed to the moss of the cooling bank. My left cheek burned dully from the wet sand at water's edge. I told my legs to stand up and they listened. What time was it? How long had I been asleep? I looked down to my watch, but there was only a bare wrist. I had forgotten my watch in the Bronco after recognizing Walker's truck. I looked up for the moon, but clouds covered the night sky. *Damn, it's dark*, I thought to myself.

There was only one thing to do; I had to start the hike out. It was far too cold to spend the whole night there. I regretted my decision to take the shortcut, since the small passage through the woods would be much darker than the main trail. Nevertheless, I stepped into the forest with outstretched hands, feeling my way through the rhododendron tunnel like I was blind.

My eyes adjusted slowly but surely, and I started making out shapes of trees and stones, black giants silhouetted against a background nearly as dark. Nothing is more dangerous than panic, and I knew these trails like a hallway in my childhood home. To the best of my ability, I controlled my breathing and tried to calm my pounding heart. One step at a time, I trudged through the night, inching toward the main trail. I saw a lighter shade of gray after I rounded the final curve of the shortcut and knew it was the opening to the main trail and a greater sense of comfort and security.

When I was ten feet away, I noticed a small shape move from the woods into the opening. I stopped dead in my tracks and waited, squinting to identify the shape. It waddled a few paces closer to where I stood. It moved awkwardly in a gait one would describe as juvenile. A series of sniffles and small grunts came next.

The moment I realized I was face to face with a black bear cub, a large stick snapped in the woods to my right, causing me to gasp and give away my position. The cub's mother let out a furious roar and started charging in my direction. As I mentioned before, the only time it's worth fearing black bears is when you are between a cub and its mother. Being as that was the precise position in which I found myself, I did the only thing I could—I ran.

Instinct told me the main trail was my best bet for putting distance between me and the bear, even though it meant running immediately by the cub. I yelled as loudly as I could and flew through the opening as the cub scurried toward its mother, who was now breaking through branches into the passage behind me. My foot slipped on the gravel of the main trail, and I fell to my knees briefly but quickly recovered and continued sprinting up the gradual incline.

I was hoping the commotion would have spooked the bear, but the protective, almost vindictive maternal instinct thrust her toward me at the speed of revenge. I knew there was nothing I could do if the bear wanted to kill me. She could run faster, climb better, and was far more powerful than I was. I kept running and hoped she would decide it wasn't worth the effort when I stopped being a threat to her cub. A heavy, terrifying canter continued to close the small distance I created.

"I could use a little hel—" I started to shout into the night in the general direction of heaven. Before I could finish the last word, my breath was knocked from me by a thundering blow to my upper back. I came crashing down onto the trail and lay motionless. My back throbbed, and I knew it would bruise, but fortunately nothing felt broken. The bear seemed to want me dead, so I played the part.

In the only stroke of fortune that day, the bear sniffed me twice and cantered back to its cub. I waited until I could hear nothing but the bats and the creek before standing up and continuing to hike. I think in a survival situation, everyone has a certain point where rather than trying to control their outcome, they resign themselves to whatever fate lies at their feet. With the combination of watching my best friend commit murder, waking up to near-freezing temperatures deep in an Appalachian Valley, and almost having my life taken by a black bear, I had reached that mental breaking point. I walked forward slowly and emotionlessly, indifferent to my surroundings. If something else tried to kill me, it was simply my time to give up the ghost.

An hour passed this way, as I methodically walked back and forth along every switchback and across every small creek crossing. I was pulled from this trance as I finally neared the parking lot by a disturbing thought. Walker would have seen my Bronco when he left the trail that afternoon. He would have known I was there. Moreover, he would have known I never found him, and being such a small creek, one can only "not find" someone intentionally. He would know. He would know that I know ... that I saw.

However, when I walked off the trail at long last, three cars were still parked at the trailhead. My Bronco, Paul's Camaro, and Walk's truck sat side by side by side, blissfully unaware of the day's events, or rather the previous day's events. A thin line of light blue was cresting the distant blue ridge horizon. Dawn was arriving. Walker must have slept in the valley with Paul's body. I stopped my mind before it could continue thinking of Walker and Paul. I still just needed to get home. I would have plenty of time—years it turned out—to deal with the fallout of what I witnessed.

When I pulled the keys out of the Bronco in our driveway, I was greeted by my frantic mother, equally as protective as the mother bear.

"Chris, honey! Where on Earth have you been? You look terrible! Are you hurt? I thought you were supposed to come home last night after fishing with Paul. I thought—"

"Mom, Mom it's okay. I'm all right." I hugged her and tried to think of an excuse. "Paul and I decided to night fish for browns on the Davidson." Paul's name tasted fetid as it left my mouth, and I winced.

"You are supposed to tell me when you do that, Chris. I was so worried about you. I called Grady, and he said Walker was fishing last night and didn't come home either. Did you see him? Were you fishing with him too?"

"No, Mom, I didn't see Walk," I lied. "We still aren't talking." At least that much was true.

"What happened to your hands? Why do you look so scratched up?"

"Oh, that's not from last night. I fell and scratched them yesterday."

She hugged me again, and I saw tears well up at the corners of her eyes. My lie made me feel sick. It was based on the premise that I knowingly disregarded my mother's sensitive feelings, something I had never done and never would do. Until I unpacked the preceding day's events, though, I could not tell her the truth, and quite honestly, the truth would more violently break her heart, as it was breaking mine.

"I'm sorry, Mom, but I need to sleep. It's been a long night." I walked past her and then past my father, who stood, but said nothing, in the doorframe of the house. I made eye contact with him as I passed, and he looked at me with an understanding that something had happened, something bad.

Chapter Fifteen

APRIL 14, 1985

THE SMELL OF spring rain permeated my room this morning, coming in from the window left ajar the night before. I pulled on the closest clothes I could find and went to the window. All was quiet outside, and for a brief moment, I wondered if I had dreamed the events of the last two days. As I felt the large bruise forming on my back, however, I realized that it had all taken place after all—the bear, the passing out, Paul and Walker.

The previous day was spent in a state of intermittent, shallow slumber and restless wandering of the mind. I wouldn't fully digest the shift in my life's course for a long time, but I had begun to realize I needed to decide what I would say if someone came asking. Once the news of Paul came to light, it would rip through town like wildfire, and my weak excuse from the previous day left more questions than answers. Why did I tell my mom

I was fishing with Paul overnight? Paul was dead, and she would soon hear of it. Where would that leave me? I had limited time to figure my story out. A day and a half was more than enough time for someone to start asking about Paul.

I realized I probably shouldn't talk to Walker, with everything going on, but at least for now, it seemed safe. For months, I had relished the idea of mine and Walker's next conversation, our reunion from the estranging events of the previous six months. I had looked forward to embracing him and affirming our friendship—our brotherhood. This is not the way I wanted it to happen. I had no feeling but dread about the idea of looking Walker Davis in the eyes and knowing my best friend was a murderer. Would he tell me the truth?

I donned a light jacket and a ball cap and left the pseudo-comfort of our home. The rain was steady that morning, drowning out the sounds of nature other than the periodic draft of air that climbed through the mountains. Normally, I would quicken my pace, so as to not linger in the weather, but I would rather be cold and soaked than force this unavoidable conversation. Would he tell me the truth?

Rather than take the trail through the cornfield, I continued down the gravel driveway until I reached the paved highway. An old Ford pickup truck flew around the corner, and without seeing me, hit the large pothole between ours and the Davises' property. Water was forcefully thrown into the air and cast in my direction, enveloping me in cold, dirty runoff. Would he tell me the truth?

I was so deep in thought, I didn't make enough noise to overpower the sound of the rain. When I walked around the corner of Grady's truck, I surprised him, and he jumped back in alarm, bracing himself against the driver's-side mirror.

"Good Lord, Chris!" was all he could muster.

"Where's Walker?"

"He's in the parlor. He's pretty torn up, Chris. Something happened yesterday when he was fishing. He seems torn up about it, but he won't tell me anything. Maybe he'll say something to you."

"I'll try to get him to talk. We haven't exactly been on good terms."

"Friends are friends. You need to put whatever this is behind you."

"I couldn't agree more. I guess you milked this morning?" I asked, changing the subject.

"Yup."

Back in the rain I went. Fortunately, the parlor was the closest structure to the house and gravel drive, as the milk truck had to access the bulk tank every week. I walked by the tank on my way into the parlor, slowly dragging my fingers across the smooth stainless steel. I remembered when Grady installed this tank, a replacement for the old one, half its size, which now collected dust in the far-off pasture's equipment shed.

I tried to remember how long ago that was ... ten, maybe fifteen years. The Altwood Dairy three miles down the road lost their contract with the processing plant due to low production. Basically, it wasn't worth their time to pick up so little product. When the contract was lost, the farm went under. Grady saw the writing on the wall and took out another agricultural loan to increase herd size. More cows necessitated a larger tank, and the silver beast was installed.

I sighed. The industry was a brutal, endless cycle of debt. As soon as a family dairy became profitable, the larger commercial dairies would get bigger, and the small farms would respond in kind with borrowed money, over and over and over.

Combine that with an outbreak of Johne's, and the writing on the wall got larger, and nearly unavoidable. Davis Milk was in trouble. Grady knew it, Walker knew it, and the whole town knew it. Images flashed into my mind of driving down the highway twenty years from now, seeing an old, rusted sign that read "Davis Milk," nearly hidden by the rebirth of nature. The farmhouse would be a leaning, dilapidated ghost of the past with shattered windows, peeling paint chips, busted floorboards. Fenceposts, if still standing, would be surrendered to the relentless growth of weeds.

Of course, none of that really seemed to matter in light of Walker's intimate encounter with the unforgiving hand of death. I wondered why I cared about the farm now. I guess deep down, my mind was still existing in the world I knew before, the world I had always known. The unbreakable bond of love for so long had fused me, Walk, and Brook.

When did I stop walking? I wondered to myself. *How long have I been standing here?* With a deep breath, I crossed both the physical and mental threshold and paced into the parlor.

Walker sat alone on the stairs leading to the front corner gate, where cows would exit after milking. His dirty face rested in the palms of his hands; elbows firmly pressed into his knees. He looked as though he hadn't showered in days. His dark curls were weighted down with grease, and instead of flipping up around the edges of his hat, they drooped somberly down his cheekbone. Further forward, a steady trickle of tears wet his cheeks before following gravity to the tip of his downward nose and dropping to the floor.

He hadn't noticed my entry, so I stood silently and waited for the right words. They never came. In fact, the right words fleetingly vanished into an unsearchable abyss of nothingness. It didn't matter. Walker shifted and produced an indecipherable, agonizing, painful cry. He furiously ripped his hat off his head and clenched it harder and harder in his fist until he couldn't bear to hold it any longer.

"Fuck!" he screamed as he threw the hat into the grime on the floor. With the hat gone, Walker's vision was no longer obstructed, and he finally noticed me standing there, mouth agape. I, likewise, finally had a clear view of his whole face. His eyes looked like hollow shells, with no trace of the hopeful, passionate, witty soul I knew. His eyelids were so red and inflamed, it seemed hard for him to keep them open. Red marks, equally spaced, streaked down his cheeks where he had apparently clawed at himself.

The eye contact with me was too much for him to bear, and he began weeping again. His shoulders bounced with each sob, and he slid down onto the ground, hands in the manure left over from Grady's early morning. I ran to him and fell at his side, wrapping my arms around him.

"Walk, it's okay, buddy. Walk, look at me. It's okay, I'm here with you." He leaned more into me with every word until I was the only thing holding him from the ground. We stayed like this for five minutes as I rubbed his back and let him release his emotions. When he finally looked up at me, some of my friend had seemed to return to his eyes.

"I don't know"—gasp—"what to do, Chris."

"Tell me what happened, Walk."

"It's Paul." He looked away, toward the side of the parlor.

"Paul? I was supposed to fish with him but spent the night with Maddy instead," I lied. He needed to tell me. I couldn't be the one to say it first.

"He ... uh ..."

"What, Walk?" I knew he was about to say it.

"Paul is dead ... he had an accident. Whenever they start talking about it—you know, on the news ... well, it's going to be wrong. No one was there to see what actually happened."

"Then what did happen? Were you with him?"

"Yeah."

"Walker, what happened?" I repeated.

"I can't talk about it with you, Chris. I'm not brave enough." Tears welled up again.

I so badly wanted to tell him that I was there, but I was having an equally hard time telling the truth. "You have to tell me."

We sat silently for what seemed like an eternity. I knew he was searching for courage. He wanted to tell me. I could feel it. When he finally looked back at me and opened his mouth, I was heartbroken and surprised at his response and moreover his change in tone.

"I just can't," he said shortly. "Besides, where have you been anyway? You haven't been here for me in months. Why should I tell you anything?"

No, Walk, don't do this, I thought. My heart started sinking. Tears began to well up in my eyes now.

"Before Paul died, he told me something about Brook. Why did he tell me? Why wasn't it you, Chris?"

Just like that, it was over. We had passed any chance of him telling me now. He was doubling down. Moreover, my suspicions were validated. Paul's stupid fucking mouth and Walk's stupid fucking emotions. I stood up.

"Well, like it or not, you're not the only one involved in this now. You dragged me into it."

"I did not," he shot back with a glare. "You're the one that lied to your mom. You got yourself into this."

"What am I supposed to say now?"

"Tell the truth, Chris. When they start asking, just tell them you were with Maddy."

"All right, buddy," I said as I placed a hand on his shoulder and turned away from him. *Maybe I will tell the truth*, I thought.

My stomach churned as I strode out of the dairy and turned back toward my house. The rain had reduced to a slow drizzle, and the birds started talking to each other, planning their day ahead. My morning had not solved any of my problems. My worst fear had been realized; Walker wasn't going to tell me what happened. The entirety of whatever resolution followed now rested heavily on my shoulders. I needed to talk to Brook.

Thirty minutes later, I was walking onto the Palmers' front porch. "Morning, Chris! Did you hear about David? Or Tom? Wait, that's not it ..." Mr. Palmer squinted his eyes and cocked his head sideways, searching for the name, or rather waiting for me to help him. I didn't have the patience for his feeble, liquored mind.

"Paul?" I asked quickly. "What about him?" My heart started to race.

"Oh yes, that's it. Paul."

"What about Paul, Mr. Palmer?"

"Well, you can go inside and see for yourself. It's all they're talking about on the news. If what they're saying is true, they found him dead this morning up in that valley in Cashiers.

"Where's Brook?" I asked without responding to his revelation.

And so it begins.

"Oh, she's here somewhere. I haven't seen her in ten minutes." He checked his watch. "Or has it been twenty?"

"Okay, thanks." I rolled my eyes and hurried past him. "I guess I'll just go find her," I mumbled under my breath. A quick survey revealed she wasn't downstairs, and I hadn't seen her on the roof when I pulled in. Either she was in her room or she had ventured into the woods. Might as well check her bedroom first.

As I climbed the stairs one at a time, I passed framed pictures of Brook and Walker, as well as Brook and her father. No pictures remained of Brook's mother, Anne. She was not much more than a figment of the imagination to Brook's father and thus was not remembered in the medium of photography. Brook never talked about her anymore. The day she chose to have an affair, whether she realized it or not, Brook's mom forfeited her relationship with her daughter. Brook always took after her father more anyway, but in her mind, her mother was truly dead to her.

Several frames up the staircase wall hung a picture from the Brevard fall dance only a few short months ago. It was a picture of the three of us. We all looked so happy, and more importantly, so innocent, despite the fact Walker was about to deck Jake. If only we could travel back to that night; that moment in time when our all-but-certain futures were laid out in front of us to take like wild blackberries from a shrub.

We could not, however, go back to that moment and instead were left with the torturous reality of the present. With a gentle, closed fist, I knocked on Brook's white bedroom door.

"Yes?" she responded.

"Are you decent?"

"Oh, Chris? Yes, I'm decent, please come in," she said.

I slowly pushed the door inward until it swung open enough to reveal my second—or potentially first, now—best friend in the world. She bounded across her room as soon as her eyes met mine and threw her arms around me. I hugged her back and held her close to my chest so that our breaths were in rhythm for a long moment. She was as in need of human contact as I was, and her body melted into my arms.

When she regained composure, she stepped back and slid her hands down my arms until they innocently held my own hands and said, "How did we find ourselves here, Chris? What's happening to all of us? We were just with Paul. Is he really dead?"

"I believe so, Brook," I responded as tears started trickling from the corners of her eyes.

"I can't believe it."

"I can't either. I just left Walker's."

"So, he knows about it too? I figured he might be working this morning and didn't see the news." She stared at me for a long time, awaiting my response.

"Brook, Walker was with Paul that day."

"What day? They found him this morning. That means it happened yesterday."

"No, I think Paul died the day before. Walker wouldn't say what happened, but he was upset."

"Wait, you were with Paul the day before!" Brook said suddenly. "After you left my house?"

"No," I lied, "I went to fish with Paul, but I couldn't find him, I guess because he met up with Walker. I ended up spending the afternoon and evening at Maddy's. I didn't come back home until yesterday morning. The only one who thinks I was with them is my mother. I told her I fished with Paul instead of admitting I slept over at Maddy's place."

"What did Walker say?" she pressed.

"He's broken, Brook. It's hard to even look at him."

"Well, I would imagine he is. Are you broken too, Chris?"

"Not yet, but honestly, I'm not far behind. I only have so much of myself stored up, and I've about given it all away. And Paul is gone. Just gone. Forever." As the words left my mouth, their gravity hit firmly on my soul. I had been in such shock about the incident that I hadn't really digested that I would never see Paul again. Yes, we had disagreements, but he was still my friend. And now one of my only friends was gone.

"Don't ever give yourself away. You have to save some for yourself, and you have to save some for me." She looked sad, obviously, but she was still Brook. That was more than could be said for Walker.

"Brook, Chris! Come down here. The police are at Walker's house. The news crew and everything is there."

"Evidence has surfaced overnight that ties Walker Davis to the location where Paul Wright's body was found," the reporter was saying as we neared the bottom of the stairs.

"Oh, no. They're going to think …" Brook said as her brain started putting the pieces together.

"Yeah," I responded. "They're going to make Walker a murder suspect. If they have pictures of his vehicle or something, he will be the last person confirmed with Paul while he was alive." I said all this very matter of fact, likely because I had already processed how this would shake itself out when I lay in bed for a whole day, scared to face the world outside my bedroom walls. It came as a devastating blow to Brook, however, who had, until moments before, no idea Walker was anywhere near Paul leading up to his death.

"They can't! He would never do something like that!" She started panicking, "You can't be serious. Chris, *please* tell me you're not being serious!"

She began to hyperventilate, so I walked her to the couch and made her sit down. We watched the television together while Walker was escorted out of the house, a county police officer on each side.

"Sources tell us that Christopher Avery was also reported to have been with Paul the night before he was found. The police did not find Avery at his home and are asking that anyone who may have information about his whereabouts or about Paul Wright come forward," the anchor continued.

"Fuck me," I said. "Why did I tell my mom I was with Paul? Damn it! And why did she have to tell the police that?"

Brook made no effort to reply. She continued to stare blankly at the screen while the reporter kept talking. "Avery's parents reportedly told the police that he left the house this morning but would be returning later this afternoon and that he would comply with law enforcement's request to come in for questioning."

"Welp, I'd better go, it seems." I grabbed Brook's hand. "Try not to worry," I told her. "This will all sort itself out." Who was I kidding? I didn't believe that for a second.

Chapter Sixteen

APRIL 15, 1985

"C'MON IN, CHRIS," a lumbering voice called through the cracked door of Sheriff Jackson's office, located at the back of the Transylvania County Sheriff's Department building. Seconds later, a recognizably weathered hand grasped the door and pushed it open.

"Hey, Grady," I said, looking up at him as he exited his interview.

"Chris?" He stopped and cocked his head to the side as a look of apprehension set upon his brow. "What are you doing here?"

"I suspect the same as you."

"Chris, you can come in now," the voice repeated, though this time with more authority. Grady shook his head, as though he were trying to shed his thoughts, and walked down the hall.

"Sheriff," I said, acknowledging the six-foot-three, 280-pound frame that sat on the opposite side of a large wooden desk in the dimly lit room.

"Sit down, Chris." I sat.

Although I had gotten into my fair share of trouble over the years in Brevard, I had never found myself in the sheriff's office. As I studied my surroundings, it became apparent how intimately connected Sheriff Jackson was with the community. The left wall was covered with pictures of him with elementary, middle, and high school baseball teams. Several trophies lined shelves on the corner bookcase. The right wall was adorned with pictures and newspaper articles displaying the sheriff with local businesses and ribbon-cutting ceremonies.

The wall immediately behind him must have been dedicated to his childhood days. From it hung black-and-white photographs of a younger Sheriff Jackson. His childhood home, his middle school football team, his high school diploma. My eyes, however, were most intently drawn to a picture that I assumed was taken after high school graduation. Jackson posed in the center of the picture with a fellow graduate on either side, all of them draped with graduation gowns and topped with mortarboards. The young man standing to the left of center was a spitting image of Walker.

"Grady," I whispered, barely audible.

"Excuse me?"

"Oh, nothing."

"Chris, do you know why you're here?"

"Yes, but what's going to happen to Walker? Where is he?"

"He is being held in jail until all this gets sorted out. Don't worry about Walker. Do you know why you're here?"

I looked away from the picture and made eye contact with the head of our local law enforcement. His dark-brown eyes were piercing—uncomfortable but not malicious. He rested his large forearms on the desk and interlocked his meaty fingers.

"You want me to make a statement about Friday."

"Your mom told Officer Greene that you were fishing with Paul Friday. Is that correct?"

"Yes, sir."

"And," he continued, "your mom said you didn't get home until Saturday morning."

"Yes, sir."

"Well Paul is dead. We have heard from Walker and his father that it was an accident, but we can't close the book on that information alone. Seeing as how you were the only other person we know was with Paul on Friday night, that makes you a person of interest. Do you catch my drift?"

"Are you saying you suspect it wasn't an accident, Sheriff?" I shifted in my seat.

"I'm not saying I suspect anything, but your statement may provide us with a little clarity on the situation, that is if you tell us the truth."

"I'm prepared to do that," I responded in earnest. I had indeed decided to tell Sheriff Jackson the truth, in part because it would vindicate me, and because I felt it was the right thing to do. Moreover, I truly believed had the roles been reversed, Walker would have told the truth.

"Good." The sheriff pushed a button on a recorder that sat in the center of his desk. I could have sworn he turned it from on to off, but I didn't say anything. After reading me my Miranda rights, he firmly said, "Tell me what happened on the evening of Friday, April 12."

I started at the beginning. I told him of my morning with Brook and my plans to fish with Paul. I elaborated on my fractured relationship with Walker and the reason he was not initially involved with our day. I described seeing both Paul's and Walker's vehicles at the trailhead and my resulting panic. When Sheriff Jackson seemed confused by that, I described in detail Brook and Walk's relationship and how Paul had seized the opportunity to make romantic moves on Brook. At this the sheriff shook his head and closed his eyes briefly.

"So, did you ever meet up with Paul on Friday?"

"Not exactly. I hiked down to the head of the waterfall on the first branch of the main valley trail. Since Paul and Walker just happened upon each other fishing in the creek, I was concerned there would be an altercation, given everything I have just told you about Brook. So, before joining them I stayed above the falls and surveyed the scene."

"And?"

"There was an altercation." I swallowed hard as the sheriff leaned in.

"You saw them fighting?" He frowned in disappointment.

"Yes, sir."

He began rubbing his forehead with one of his oversized hands. I leaned forward and laid my arm on the desk, letting my head rest on it, facedown partly to avoid his gaze, but also to hide the tears that were wetting my eyelids. *Here we go*, I thought after a long pause.

"Sheriff Jackson," I gasped as I searched for the words, "Paul picked up a rock and tried to hit Walker. He missed and hit Walk's arm. And then ..." I choked. "And then Walker took the stone—"

"That's all I needed to know, Chris."

Not hearing or comprehending what he said I continued, "and he beat Paul in the head—"

"*Chris, enough!*"

"What ...?" I asked in confusion. "I don't understand. I'm telling you what happened." I wiped tears from
my cheeks, and my breathing began to recover.

"All I need to know now, Chris, is if Walker or Paul
saw you?"

"No sir, but I—"

"And did either of them see your Bronco at the
trailhead?"

I couldn't believe the calmness of his voice. Did
he not understand what I was trying to tell him? Why
would he stop me?

"No, sir. Walk's truck was there when I left the next
morning. I think he slept somewhere on the trail. But
sir, I—"

"Listen to me carefully, Chris. Walker said you weren't
in Lonesome Valley Friday night. Do you understand?"

"No, I don't understand at all, actually. I was told
to come make a statement, and it's taken me several days
to work up the courage to do so." My confusion was
quickly being replaced with irritation.

"And for that, we are appreciative. But I'm serious,
Chris. I know all I need to know now. You can leave. We
are done here," he said as he gestured toward the door. I
looked at the picture of young Sheriff Jackson and Grady
on the wall and started to realize what was going on.

"I know what I saw," was the only sentence I could muster.

"Well, you'd best forget it. They were fishing near a waterfall, and Paul slipped. Accidents like that happen all the time. The last thing this town and its residents need is some fancifully spun drama based on one witness. Besides, seeing as how Walker is your best friend, it seems fortunate nothing more will come of this." His eyes narrowed, and we both looked at each other for several seconds without blinking.

"Let me remind you that other than Walker, you were the last person to see Paul. If this whole incident gets drawn out too much, you may find yourself getting pulled into it one way or another." The threat was not overly veiled. "Walker said you spent the night with Maddy. He said that the only reason you told your mom you had been with Paul is to cover up your evening away from home with a girl. Isn't that what happened?"

"I, uh ..."

"Chris, is that or isn't it what happened?"

"Yes, sir." I said quietly. "I guess that's what happened." As much as I wanted something more to come from my telling the truth, I was frankly terrified of Sheriff Jackson, and I certainly didn't want to get pulled into any investigation. Maybe things would be better this way. After all, we would be more likely to get Walker back.

I stood up and left the room without any final acknowledgment. When I stepped out into the warm spring sun at the front of the station, several birds lifted from a bench and flew off in search of a safer perch. I walked over to the bench and collapsed onto it. Regardless of the nature of my conversation with the sheriff, the weight of my secret had been lifted. No longer would I have to bear the burden of my conscience. I told the truth; or tried anyway. What happened next was out of my control.

Is he really just that close to Grady? I thought. *Does Grady know what happened? Had Walk told him?* It was clear that Sheriff Jackson was going to cover it up. I was the only witness, and he gave me an alibi. I wouldn't even have to convince Maddy to go along with it. Obviously, Paul was a transplant from Charleston and didn't have ties to Brevard like Walk and Grady, but I couldn't fathom covering up murder, accident or not.

I didn't understand why he would want me to come in for questioning if he heard I had been with Paul, unless he wanted to find out if there would be any loose ends. He must have wanted to see if anyone knew anything more than Walker's story. Well, now he knew; I made damned sure of that.

What of Paul's family? Would they believe it? I imagined the utter horror they must be going through right now. Maybe their sorrow would cloud some of the details of their son's passing. Do they even know who Walker is? Had Paul told them about Brook? There were so many questions, and I started feeling dizzy. I tried to take a deep breath and enjoy the sun on my skin, but my mind wouldn't stop churning.

As if on cue, a disheveled man and woman came racing up the sidewalk toward the sheriff's department. The gentleman was tall, blond-haired, and blue-eyed, and wore an expensive suit. His stride was long and determined, and he was so fixated on the door of the station, he never even glanced in my direction as he passed. His wife walked closely behind him and seemed to be blotting her eyes with a lace handkerchief. They stuck out like sore thumbs.

Paul's parents, I thought to myself as I sat upright on the bench. I couldn't leave now. I had to wait and see what happened.

I wasn't long idle. Less than ten minutes after they entered the station, the Wrights reappeared in a furious frenzy, followed closely by an agitated Sheriff Jackson. Once through, Dr. Wright slammed the heavy wooden door in the sheriff's face. It was flung open as aggressively as it was closed.

"I'm telling you guys, there is nothing more I can do! I am—we all are—heartbroken for your loss and will extend whatever help you may need, but this looks like an accident. The young man has already been arrested, and there will be a trial. I can't do anything else about it right now."

"Oh, this was no accident," Mrs. Wright growled through clenched teeth. "I saw his bloody, beaten skull. And I've heard of this Walker Davis before. His drinking habits, his anger, his instability! He's a poor farmer's kid from nowhere. He's *trash*! I know he did this to our son!"

"I personally know Walker and his father, Grady, Mrs. Wright, and I can assure you they are good, upstanding, Christian citizens. Don't turn your sorrow into aimless accusations. I'll not hear it."

"Oh, but you will hear it. You'll hear it from the attorney. This story smells like shit, and you know it. And of *course* you know them," Mr. Wright said as he turned away, grabbing his wife's hand.

"Damn it!" Sheriff Jackson said before finally noticing me, his audience, quietly seated on the bench. "Not a word, Chris! Not a Goddamned word."

I pondered the sheriff's threat. He couldn't keep me from talking to Paul's parents. Whether or not that was something I wanted to do was another question entirely.

Chapter Seventeen

APRIL 16, 1985

THE DAY AFTER I left the sheriff's office with a force-fed alibi, Walker was indicted by a grand jury and formally admitted to the Transylvania County Detention Center to await an arraignment date. Grady, who was struggling to keep the dairy afloat, now without his only farmhand, could not make bail, and thus Walker was bound to sit alone in a cell with nothing but his thoughts and a heavy conscience.

I stumbled out of bed at four thirty in the morning that morning and walked over to my small oak dresser that sat below the window on the exterior wall of the room. I pulled out a pair of faded blue jeans and struggled to pull them on, as the heavy fog of tiredness slowed the pathway from my brain to my hands. I would have loved nothing more than to continue slumbering, since I lay awake half of the night, but there was something else I needed to do that morning. I looked out into the black of night and saw a faint glow on the far side of the cornfield. Grady.

The previous night, after eating a late dinner of spaghetti and meatballs that my mother prepared, I decided to wander through the woods for a while to clear my mind. When I neared the border to the Davises' property, I heard the groan of Grady's large tractor making its way to the far-off pasture. The sun was beginning to set behind the mountains in the west.

Poor Grady, I had thought to myself, knowing well that he had been working around the dairy since four in the morning and was still struggling to feed cows after the sun had set, only to get up and do the entire thing again the next day, and the next day, and the next day; all without Walker to help him. The school year was finishing up, and I had done well enough that spring to coast into graduation, no matter how I performed on my final exams. My parents told me not to worry about making money for a while, since they didn't want to add to my plate, but I couldn't sit around with my thoughts. It would leave me in no better current position than Walker. That night, looking out through the trees at the tractor's headlights, I decided I would spend the next few weeks helping Grady.

After getting dressed, I walked out into the warming early morning air and started making my way toward the parlor and the rhythmic clicking noise produced by the pumps. I thought of the few times I helped Walker milk during the winter, making me thankful for the mild temperatures of this April, especially after the cold of March. When I emerged from the cornfield trail opening onto the dairy's gravel driveway, I heard the familiar sound of Grady's pleading shouts, begging the cows to move into the parlor to be milked. I laughed to myself at some of the novel, explicit phrases being released into the otherwise quiet and peaceful surroundings.

I walked up to the holding area between the milk barn and the parlor and joined Grady in pushing cows forward. "C'mon, girls! Get up! Move up!" I walked from side to side behind them, gesturing toward the open hydraulic gateways on either side. Grady looked up when he heard my voice and gave a sigh of relief. He walked down the staircase made for people into the recessed center aisle of the milking room and waited until I had moved six Holsteins into each side of the parlor before pressing the button to close them in.

"Boy, am I happy to see you," he said, raising his eyebrows at me. He was dripping sweat from every angular surface of his body.

"It's the least I could do."

I claimed the right side of the parlor while Grady worked with the cows on the left side. One by one, starting at the front, we disinfected the cows' udders with betadine and attached a four-claw cluster pump to all four teats. After attaching the last pump to the sixth cow I watched the bell, a plastic hub where the claws of the pumps join, start filling with milk. Milking cows is therapeutic. Something about the thought-drowning sound of the parlor, the suctioning attachment of pumps to cows, the pure white liquid filling the bell and traveling through pipes to the bulk tank in the next room. Dairy cows can be milked for many months to even over a year after they calve if they are milked twice a day. If they aren't properly milked out, their mammary tissue—or bags—become swollen, painful, and can get infected with mastitis. Part of the joy of milking is knowing the relief you are giving these beautiful creatures.

Once the first group was milked for several minutes, the pumps automatically started falling off and were hung back up on hooks that extended from above. After the last cow finished giving milk, Grady pressed a button to open the front gates of the parlor, allowing the cows to leave and walk down an enclosed tunnel back into the milk barn to eat their breakfast.

Grady and I repeated this cycle for several hours, using mostly hand signals to communicate with each other and loud shouts to instruct the cows where to go. Dairy cattle are not scared of people in the same way as beef cattle and thus require more verbal beckoning to get them moving. Yelling at them is not malicious, and I never saw Grady put an abusive hand on any of his animals. Many of his cows were just plain stubborn.

At seven thirty, we returned the final group of cows to the barn and started cleaning the parlor, scrubbing each surface inch by inch to remove milk, betadine, and manure. The pipe from the bulk tank was lifted, and the pumps were finally turned off, allowing us to hear each other while we toiled.

"How are you doing, Grady? You hanging in there?" I asked after building up the courage to broach the subject on both of our minds.

"I just," he started, setting his brush down to look at me, "I just don't know why they have to keep him locked up when it was clearly an accident. Walker is the best kind of kid there is. If he says Paul fell, then Paul fell! They don't have any real evidence. Both of their cars were there because they were fishing together. What do they expect?"

I thought about what he said before responding. After my conversation with Sheriff Jackson, I half-expected Grady to know what actually happened. I thought Walker might have told his father, but it seemed as though he did not. Jackson must have suspected there was more to Walker's story and took it upon his own initiative to try to protect his old friend. Grady had no idea what his son did that day, and I so badly hoped he would never find out. *Man, what a dumb move by Jackson*, I thought.

"I think it's just procedure," I said. "He was the last one with Paul and the only witness." My stomach churned. "If he's innocent, the court system will prove that."

"Of course, he's innocent! I hope this is over soon." Grady pulled off his hat and wiped his forehead with the back of his hand, leaving a dark streak of dirt behind. "I can't keep doing this, Chris. I'm too old for this shit. It's all I can do to get out of bed every morning, knowing everything I have to do around here."

"I'm here to help you. I can keep coming until this whole thing is over."

"I appreciate it, but I don't have the money to pay you. You need to go get a proper job."

"I don't want one. I have enough put away to be okay for a little while. Besides, I'm living at home, and Mom cooks every night. I don't really have to spend any money right now."

"Still, Chris, I can't let you do that."

"I'm doing it. This is where I want to be. You'll have to teach me how to drive the tractor, though. I've never done that."

"If you can drive your Bronco, you can drive the tractor. It's easy." He stopped and looked at me for a prolonged moment, studying. "Okay, fine. If you really want to help, I sure could use it."

An hour later, I was driving the tractor like I had done it my whole life, the heavy mixing wagon in tow, on my way to feed cows on pasture. Despite being tired, I felt like I was doing the right thing, and it took my mind off the heavy burden on my heart and soul.

The sun was still on the horizon when we put the equipment away for the day, much to Grady's delight. "Thanks for your help today, Chris. It made such a big difference."

"You don't have to thank me."

"Oh, I almost forgot to tell you, Walker's arraignment is tomorrow. He told me he wants you to be there. Thought you'd like to know."

I guess he still cares about me, after all.

Chapter Eighteen

APRIL 17, 1985

I PEELED OFF a large flap of skin from a blister on my palm as I waited for Brook to climb in the Bronco. *That'll add some fun to work this week*, I thought as I winced at the sharp pain.

"Sorry, Dad was in quite a state this morning," Brook said as she slammed the heavy passenger side door and began cranking the window closed.

"No worries, I told you it was at nine so we might make it on time at nine thirty."

Brook didn't notice my quip but instead looked flustered.

"How are you feeling about everything?" I asked her as we started making our way to the courthouse downtown.

"I don't know. I'm just ready for it to start so it can be over faster."

"Me too," I responded.

"Do you think they will charge him with murder?" she asked quietly.

"I do. I have heard rumors the autopsy findings are pretty bad for Walk."

"You don't think," she started, looking away from me out her window, "he could actually have done it? Killed Paul?"

"I don't think so." I kept my gaze on the road so that I wouldn't have to lie directly to her innocent, trusting face.

"I mean, what if Paul told him about kissing me or something?"

I winced. Fortunately, Brook was still looking in the other direction. "I mean, I don't know, Brook. What do you want me to say? It's Walker. I don't think he'd be capable of killing someone. At least, not on purpose."

"But he always got in fights? What if ... what if—"

"Brook, please. I don't want to think about that. Either way, he is going to stand trial for murder. A jury will have to decide if he did it, not us." I turned the dial on the radio to break the awkwardness of the moment.

We drove the rest of the way to town having little more than small talk. As we passed over the Davidson River, I looked down from the bridge and watched as a younger, probably high-school-aged, kid completed his final motion of a double haul, sending his fly, invisible to me, toward the rhododendron-laden bank. What I would give to join him and fish. Instead, I found myself still grasping at fractured pieces of the naïve world we all were forced to abandon.

When we pulled into the parking lot of the courthouse, I spotted Grady's truck and parked next to it. He, still waiting in the driver's seat, tipped his hat to us, and we all got out to walk to the front of the building.

"Well, I think we all know where this is going, but let's try to be positive for Walker," Grady said. His eyes rested on heavy bags, and I noticed dried salt around his eyelids.

"Let's also be positive for each other," I added.

"All rise. Court is now in session. The Honorable Mason Whitaker presiding." The bailiff's voice echoed through the mostly empty courtroom. "Let's pray." All heads in the room bowed. "Almighty God, we stand here today in Your presence as our Supreme Judge and ask that You may lead us in accordance to Your will. Give us the clarity of mind and the fullness of heart and spirit that are required to find truth, peace, and justice. Guide us in the path of righteousness that befits Your great glory. Amen."

Judge Whitaker, a slender, balding man with a wispy ring of fine white hair, strolled into the room and took his seat at the bench. "Court is in session," he said as he stamped the gavel, "Call the case, please."

"For arraignment, People of the State of North Carolina versus Walker Graydon Davis for violation of subchapter three, article six, G. S. fourteen to seventeen A, committing homicide," the clerk said loudly.

I squeezed Brook's hand.

"Appearance for prosecution and the defense," he continued.

"Your Honor, I am attorney Horace Batton, appearing as a public prosecutor," a voice responded from the other side of the aisle. I realized I had not paid any attention to anyone in the room other than Walker, Brook, and Grady. I took the time to study the prosecuting district attorney. Mr. Batton was recently gaining fame, or infamy depending on who you asked, for his dealing with a homicide in Winston-Salem that was prosecuted in Raleigh earlier that spring, a case that was fresh in all our minds for being the first capital punishment sentencing in almost five years. He was short, shrewd, and professional. He was known for being blunt and direct. He wore a dark-brown three-piece suit. Small stubble of hair clung tightly to the back of his scalp. His eyes were small, dark, and piercing, though partially hidden behind thick-rimmed glasses.

"And the defense?"

"Your Honor, I am attorney Benjamin Johnson, defense counsel for the accused." I turned my attention toward the author of these words, Walker's state-provided attorney. He was a rather ordinary-looking man, younger than his counterpart, with a full head of combed brown hair. *He certainly seems more likeable than Batton*, I thought to myself. I wondered how much Walker had told him about April 12. Being uneducated in legal proceedings, I didn't know if Walker would have the freedom to share the actual events of the day with his attorney and still plead not guilty. Then another thought popped into my head, *Maybe Walker decided to tell the truth.*

"Is the accused here?" Judge Whitaker asked.

"Yes, Your Honor. Mr. Davis, please approach the bench," the clerk responded.

Walker slowly walked to the front of the courtroom, hands in his pockets.

"Mr. Davis, you have chosen to be represented by a state-provided attorney. Is that correct?"

"Yes sir, I will be represented by Mr. Johnson." Walker responded.

"Very well. Will the clerk please swear in the accused?"

I leaned over and whispered in Brook's ear, "This is it. Almost done."

"Please raise your right hand. Do you swear to tell the truth, the whole truth, and nothing but the truth?"

"Yes sir, I do."

The clerk cleared his throat. "Accused Walker Graydon Davis commits crime of homicide. That on the twelfth of April 1985 in Transylvania County, North Carolina, and within the jurisdiction of this Honorable Court, the accused committed murder in the second degree."

Brook softly sniffled, and I looked over to see her crying. I wiped a large tear on her left cheek away with my finger. "Be strong," I whispered in her ear.

The judge sat back in his chair. "Do you understand the crime charged against you?"

"Yes, Your Honor." Walker's voice sounded firm, strong, and perhaps rehearsed.

"What is your plea?"

I leaned forward. *Does he do it?*

"Not guilty, Your Honor."

Nope.

Judge Whitaker stood up. "Let it be on the record that the accused pleaded not guilty for the crime of murder in the second degree and that attorney Benjamin Johnson assisted him in this arraignment."

Horace Batton rose to his feet to match the movement by Judge Whitaker. "Your Honor, we would like to set the case for pretrial on May 20, 1985."

"Mr. Davis and Mr. Johnson, are you amenable with the schedule?" the judge asked.

"Yes, Your Honor," replied Johnson.

"No objections both for prosecution and defense. The case is set for pretrial conference on May 20, 1985. Notify the parties thereto. So ordered."

As the clerk adjourned the court, I watched Walker turn and search the room. When his gaze landed on me, he stopped and held eye contact. For some reason, I started feeling chills. Even from afar, I could see kindness and friendship in his eyes. The voices around us faded into the background as we communicated the feelings in both our hearts without words. I let the stress of the murder and the trial be momentarily forgotten and held my gaze on my best friend in the world. Years of memories swirled in my mind, each bringing emotions—happiness, hopefulness, sorrow, love. I felt tears start building in my eyes.

"Chris." The voice was quiet at first. "Chris!" Louder now. "Hey, Chris!" A hand shook my shoulder.

Realizing it was Grady, I turned away from Walker. "What, Grady?"

"Where did Brook go?"

I looked around the courtroom. The seat next to me was empty. "I don't know. I never saw her leave."

"Let's go find her. She looked upset toward the end there," Grady said, as he beckoned me to walk down the aisle toward the back of the courtroom.

I looked back toward Walker once more, but he was talking with his attorney.

When we stepped outside into the moist spring air, I searched my surroundings but only saw several passers-by and a lone reporter scribbling something down on a notepad. I turned to Grady. "You walk around the left side of the building. I'll go right. She's got to be around here somewhere."

Grady nodded and started making his way to the corner of the building.

I flushed a rabbit as I paced along the side wall. Had Brook come this way, the rabbit would likely have already fled her passing. I hurriedly made my way around the back of the building until I met up with Grady, whose luck hadn't been any better, evidenced by his pressed lips and slow head shake.

"Damn, you think she went home?" Grady asked.

"Not without a car."

The smell of barbecue drifted out of the wind, reminding me of the previous summer, sitting atop the

water tower with Paul, Brook, and Walker. In reminisc-
ing, my glance turned toward the old, dilapidated tower
at the end of the street. A small figure was making its way
up the ladder toward the platform.

"The water tower ..." I said as I started down the
street. Grady recognized the figure as well and followed.

"Brook!" I shouted as I reached the bottom of the
rusted structure. "Come down, Brook. Let's go home."

"What's the point, Chris?" she sobbed.

"Please, Brook. It's broad daylight. Let's go somewhere else!"

"I'm not coming down!"

"Then would you mind if we came up?" I asked.
Grady made a face as to say, *You expect me to climb up that
rickety ladder?*

Brook shrugged.

I ascended the old ladder first so that I could
help pull Grady onto the platform. Brook shifted but
remained seated, holding her legs close to her chest, gently rocking back and forth. Grady and I approached her
and took a seat on either side. Our arms collided as we
simultaneously put them around her shoulders. Words
were postponed as we sat and let Brook cry out her emotions for what seemed like half an hour.

"I don't know what to say." Brook finally broke the
silence. "Murder ..."

"They don't have any evidence. Surely, he won't be convicted," I replied, feeling a deep discomfort in the pit of my belly.

"We know he didn't do anything. The jury will know that too," Grady added. "Innocent until proven guilty."

"Regardless of what really happened, all the prosecution has to do is convince a jury. And we all know Walk," Brook said. She was right, of course. Everyone in Brevard had been witness to Walker's character this spring. The drinking, the emotional outbursts, the irrationality. Moreover, everyone knew the dairy was in trouble. None of this would help Walker in the eyes of a jury.

"We can't think about that now. All that's happened is an arraignment. This will be a long and thorough process, and we have to hope Walker will be acquitted, for our sanity and for his." I grabbed Brook by her shoulder and turned her to face me. "Brook, don't borrow trouble. Today has enough of its own."

We sat with our legs dangling in the Appalachian breeze for the rest of the morning, watching heavy scattered clouds pass overhead on their journey east to bring life to the dense mountain canopies. The clear morning horizons of March had retreated and were replaced by the somewhat hazy air of an unnaturally warm April. The mountains in the distance, though visible, had mottled edges as if they were merely a watercolor painting of their true selves. In that moment, I felt an unnatural call to join them, to see their true beauty and wonder, to explore their virgin creeks, to climb the lonely sycamores, to sleep on a soft bed of white pine needles deep in the forest.

    Soon, I hoped.

Chapter Nineteen

MAY 18, 1985

THE PRELIMINARY HEARING came and went. Unfortunately for Walker, there was enough burden of
persuasion for the prosecution to satisfy Judge Whitaker
to move forward with the case and the set a pretrial date
of May 20. Despite our moment at the arraignment, I had
not built the courage to face Walker yet. Grady seemed
rather quiet about all of it during the days spent helping
him around the dairy. I assumed that meant it wasn't
looking good for Walker, so I didn't ask how discovery
sessions and the numerous conferences were going. We
had enough work to do that it left little time for talking
anyway.

In the month since Paul Wright's death and
Walker's indictment, the town of Brevard became
charged with polarizing energy and emotion. As the
pretrial date neared, some of the town's feelings boiled

over. One of the catalysts was an event Maddy and I stumbled upon after seeing a film at the small theater downtown two days before May 20. We left the theater around nine in the evening and began to walk toward the Bronco, which was a quarter mile away in a small parking lot on Broad Street near campus. As we neared the lot, we saw a crowd of a couple hundred people in a field outside the college. The crowd was dotted with small lights that we realized were candles.

I had a feeling I already knew what the event was, but for some reason, I looked at Maddy and said, "Let's go see what's going on." I took her hand and led her across the road and toward the low murmur of voices. As we approached, we started noticing faces we knew, mostly students from school. Each time I tried to make eye contact with what I thought were my friends, they turned quickly away or looked at the ground. We continued through the crowd, ignoring the cold glances, and made our way toward the small stage set up in the middle.

Voices died down, and I saw Paul's father walk onto the platform.

"Does anyone else have anything they would like to say?" he yelled loudly over the crowd.

Jake, the same kid who had made a move on Maddy at the dance and was subsequently knocked to the ground by Walker, pushed through the edge of the crowd and walked up onto the stage. "I would like to say a few words." He waited until no one was speaking. "Paul was a good friend of mine." *A lie.* "I had several classes with him and got to know him real well over the course of this last year. I think everyone here loved Paul." Several people in the crowd vocally agreed. "And I can't believe what happened to him. Let me clarify, I think we all *know* what happened to him. I just can't believe anyone thinks it was an accident!" More people agreed angrily, causing Maddy and me to look at each other and start backing up.

"Walker is a murderer!" one voice said loudly from the left side of the stage. Several *yeah*s and *that's right*s were shouted.

"We need to get out of here," Maddy said desperately as she started pulling me toward the back of the crowd. I followed her closely, but she soon stopped. When I looked to see why, my blood started boiling. Classmates of ours were intentionally getting in our way.

A red-haired girl named Susan glared at us and hissed, "Where do you think you're going?" Maddy looked to me for help. "You should stay and hear this. You're his best friend, after all."

"Please just let us leave," I begged, stepping in front of Maddy, who was trembling.

"Walker is a murderer!" she said loudly. People who had yet to see us started taking notice when they heard Susan, causing the small clearing around us to start shrinking.

"We are leaving!" I shouted as I started to push past people. Susan followed us and smacked my keys out of my hand. When I leaned over to pick them up, someone I didn't even recognize kicked my leg out from under me, causing me to fall. I grabbed my keys off the grass and exploded to my feet, knocking several people back. Maddy had used the moment of chaos to make a break for the road. I ran after her, ignoring the shoulders I violently jolted on my way behind her.

Maddy was crying when I reached her, hands on her knees in the middle of Broad Street. "C'mon, sweet girl," I said as I took hold of her forearms. She stood, and we walked with my arm around her shoulder back to the Bronco. I kissed her cheek and whispered, "It's going to be okay," before I shut her door and walked around to the driver's side. I dropped her off a few minutes later and drove home, depressed by how our night had ended. Happy moments had been hard to come by lately, and I had hoped to provide one that evening for Maddy. I failed.

We weren't the only ones picked on that night. When I arrived at the dairy the next morning, my first job was to clean eggs off Grady's house and the barn closest to the road. Grady must not have noticed when he left for the feed store after milking. I was hoping to be finished by the time he got home. Unfortunately, he was back just in time to see me scrubbing the last bit of yolk and shell off the front porch. It gave me great joy, however, when Grady told me Jake's father's hardware store had busted windows.

Chapter Twenty

MAY 20, 1985

My body bounced in the seat as I throttled the tractor down a gear to climb up a small, graded hill back onto the gravel driveway. I turned around to watch the mixing wagon follow the tractor as the trailer hitch almost bottomed out on the precipice of the hill. *Damn, need to take a different angle next time.* Now that the last of the pasture cows were fed their mixed ration, it was time to attach the bale fork and start moving hay into the pastures.

Before pulling into the equipment shed, I engaged the brake and jumped off, leaving the tractor idling behind me. Grady walked out of the back door of his house, dressed in a faded, gray three-piece suit and freshly combed hair.

"You look good," I said loudly, competing with the rumbles of the engine behind me.

"Thanks!" Grady shouted in return. "Thanks for doing this. If the tractor hadn't broken down, we'd have moved the hay yesterday, like we planned."

"It's no problem. Let me know how it goes!"

"Oh, I will! If everything goes as planned, McClung will be out of the picture." The corners of Grady's lips turned up into a subdued, closed-mouth smile.

Grady was referring to the biggest development in Walker's case since his arraignment. The previous day, Brook's father had called the dairy, frantic and surprisingly sober. Mid-morning, when I was passing in front of the calf barn, Grady waved me toward him, his body hanging out of the door and a phone cord trailing back into the house.

When I reached the steps leading up to the flaking white doorframe, I heard Grady talking excitedly. "Are you sure? You have to be positive!" He paused, and I heard an emphatic but muffled response come through the speaker on the phone. "I'll be damned. We can use that! The pretrial is tomorrow! You just gave us what we needed. I'll call you back if I have any other questions. All right, thanks again." He hung up the phone and leaned against the door.

"What's going on, Grady? What is it?"

"McClung!"

"The medical examiner? What about him?"

"He's friends with the Wrights! That was Mr. Palmer on the phone. He's from Charleston and knew the Wrights, obviously—he was the one that introduced y'all to Paul. He said they graduated from MUSC with Dr. McClung."

"Oh my God! Grady, you know what that m—"

"We can try to get him thrown out of the trial! It's a conflict of interest. He could have made the whole thing up. They buried the body a month ago!"

"We can do it tomorrow!"

Grady smiled widely as he embraced a large dose of hope about his son's future.

The next day, I stood there, wishing Grady luck getting a witness for the prosecution thrown out, even though I knew what the medical examiner found was real; I watched it happen. I watched as the stone in Walker's hand impacted Paul's fragile temple, breaking his skull and killing him. I watched Walker hold Paul's lifeless body, convulsing, moaning, and begging God to bring him back. I watched my best friend murder another friend. Of course, I never told any of that to Grady.

"Good luck, Grady. I hope to be done with the hay when you get back."

"All righty, then, here goes nothing!" Grady loaded into his farm truck and flew down the driveway, kicking up a cloud of dust.

An hour later, I was returning to the hay field to fork another bale. My conscience felt like it was splitting at the seams, and it was hard to concentrate on my job. *Will I be haunted by this for the rest of my life? If he walks, I will have helped cover up a murder.* I was already haunted by it, and it wasn't going to get better with time, not something like that. But I couldn't bring myself to do anything about it.

I was scared of the sheriff. He was right, I was with Walker and Paul, in a way. He's the only one who knows my real story. If I disobeyed him and started talking, he could easily drag me into the trial, not as a witness, but as a suspect—an accessory to murder. I never told anyone else where I was on April 12. I never had to tell Maddy I used her as an alibi, since the sheriff kept me away from questioning. On top of that, the town seemed to have turned against me, evidenced by the night of the candlelight vigil. I didn't want to be anywhere near that trial. I also wanted my friend back. It would be different, of course, but I hoped with time it could go back to normal.

I was so busy battling my own emotions, I hadn't noticed how soft the ground had gotten under the open gate leading into the largest pasture after repeatedly pushing the tractor over it. I was pulled from my thoughts when I felt the back wheels slip. *Shit*, I thought. I looked down beside me to see six inches of mud being churned up by the wide tire treads. I dropped gears and revved the engine. The tires slipped again, then once more. The fourth time they slipped, the tires continued spinning on their own, and the tractor stood still.

"Ugh, just what I needed right now!" I started quickly moving the steering wheel back and forth, trying my best to get the tires to establish grip. I didn't realize it was possible to get a tractor this size stuck in the mud. After giving it every effort for fifteen minutes I gave up and jumped down into the thick mud. Fortunately, there was enough room to close the pasture gate. "Well, at least they have *some* hay."

I approached the house on foot as Grady pulled into the driveway. When he was close enough for me to see his face through the windshield, I realized the pretrial hadn't gone well. I waited for him to come to a stop. He opened the door and stepped out.

"Well?" I asked.

Grady rubbed the back of his neck and shook his head in clear disappointment. "Can't do it. They're still going to use the autopsy."

Great, and now I have to tell him about the tractor too.

Chapter Twenty-One

JULY 23, 1985

"**ARE YOU READY?**" I asked as I finished my last sip of English breakfast tea and stood up from the formal Charlestonian chaise longue in the Palmers' study.

"I will never be ready," she said softly.

"We have to try." I took Brook's hand and squeezed it with affection.

"All right, I'm ready enough, I guess."

The boards of the porch and steps groaned as we made our way toward the Bronco. The first day of the trial was oppressively hot and humid. My scalp started to sweat during the brief walk to the vehicle. I opened the passenger door for Brook and hugged her firmly. When I released the embrace, she turned forward and stared directly ahead as if to say, *Let's get this over with.*

"What are you going to do after the trial? I mean, honestly, Chris, it's July. You have to think about your future. For better or worse, this nightmare will be over in a matter of weeks. Where does that leave you?"

"Where does it leave you?" I returned her question.

"I don't know. I mean, if he is acquitted, I'll talk it all out with him."

"After everything, you'll run right back to Walker." I meant it as a question, but it came out as a defeated, resigned statement.

"I love him, Chris. I'll always love him, and it's not something I can change. I feel like I'm in a burning house and love is the very air I breathe. It's full of smoke and each breath sears my lungs, but with each breath is hope that I will be pulled from the fire. To stop breathing is to give up, to die. To stop loving Walker is to give up, to ..."

"And you lecture me," I said, cutting a judging glance at her.

"I can't help how I feel."

"Well, for my sake try, Brook. You have more to live—excuse me, to breathe for—than Walker Davis."

"You never answered me. What are *you* going to do after the trial?"

"I don't know. My parents think I should go to Charleston after all. I can't imagine leaving this place." I glanced out of the window and looked at the ridges of layered green, marking the edge of our valley.

"I know you love it here, but you have to do what's best for you. Your parents are probably right."

There was nowhere to park outside the courthouse, so we were forced to leave the Bronco up the street near the bakery. As we walked down the road, we were both shocked at the sheer number of people in our small town. White vans with different news channel logos lined the street for several blocks. Reporters congregated on the front lawn and stopped anyone who would submit to interviewing.

"Yeah, I know Walker. You know his nickname, right? 'Smokes.' Walker 'Smokes' Davis," some nerdy underclassman was saying to one of the reporters as we walked past. I glared at him, but he continued, "They call him that because he—"

"You're wasting your time," I said to the reporter.

"Excuse me, what is your name, son?" the greasy, wig-wearing reporter asked, turning to me and Brook. "Can we talk with you for a moment?" He gestured to his cameraman to point it toward me.

"No, you may not," Brook replied. "C'mon, let's go inside." She tugged at my arm. We walked inside, and I seated her next to Grady.

The courtroom was abuzz with energy. As I looked around, I saw most of our classmates in attendance and recognized many faces from around town. I tried not to hold eye contact with anyone for too long, as I was still unsettled by my and Maddy's recent interactions with classmates.

One interaction I welcomed eagerly, however, was with Clyde from the fly shop. He hobbled over toward my direction from the front of the room. I met him half-way and shook his weathered, firm hand.

"Did you hear?" he asked.

"Hear what?"

"I'm testifying for Walker today as a character witness. That's a good kid right there, and these people ought to know it."

"No, I didn't hear that," I said regretfully. "Grady didn't tell me." In reality, I hadn't asked. I was so afraid to get pulled into the trial, I feared even asking about it might elicit an invitation from Grady to be a character witness myself. I was honestly a little surprised Walker didn't ask to have me testify.

"Did you see what happened to Atwell Hardware?" he asked, referring to Jake's father's store that had been vandalized. "It's such a shame, isn't it." He grinned and winked at me.

"Clyde! Aren't you supposed to be with the other witnesses or something?"

When Clyde returned to where he was sitting, I walked to the front of the room and found Walker, who was about to take his place at the defense table.

"Hey, buddy," I said as I approached him.

"Chris," he replied.

"You look like hell."

"Yeah, well the jail ain't exactly a resort."

I looked around to make sure no one important cared that I was talking with him. "I miss you, Walk."

The bailiff walked toward me from the other side of the room, surely about to tell me to be seated.

"Come visit me tonight," Walker said, grabbing my forearm. "I want to talk to you about something."

"Okay. I'll be there."

After sitting down next to Brook, I took the opportunity to study the jurors. I was disappointed, but not surprised, to see no familiar faces. On the far left was an older man, with an unkempt beard and a loosely fitting blazer. He looked like a farmer, or maybe he just reminded me of Grady. Moving from him in order from left to right was a middle-aged woman, a young professional man, an older Black lady, another likely farmer, a young red-haired woman, a wrinkled, grayed woman, and lastly a round, stumpy-looking man with a red face. *This will all depend on them*, I thought to myself.

Shortly after initial formalities, the trial proceeded. The chief prosecutor for the North Carolina Grand Jury, District Attorney Horace Batton, began the prosecution's opening statements.

"Your Honor, ladies and gentlemen of the jury, today the good people of North Carolina are charging Walker Davis with violating subchapter three, article six, G. S. fourteen to seventeen a. The prosecution is charging Walker Davis with the willful second-degree murder of Paul Wright on April 12, 1985. The people will prove beyond a reasonable doubt that Paul Wright was killed by Walker Davis by calling forth to the stand four witnesses." I looked at Brook, sitting once again by my side and shrugged. *Four witnesses. It didn't seem like too many.*

Batton continued, "First to the stand will be Stephen Moore, who provided photographic evidence of Walker Davis's vehicle parked alongside Paul Wright's vehicle at the Lonesome Valley trailhead the morning of April 13, when it was realized Paul was missing. He was, of course, found dead the next day in the Lonesome Valley.

"Secondly, we will call on Jake Atwell—" Jake Atwell? Was he still that upset about Walker kicking his ass? My face began feeling hot as I fumed over the name. "—as a character witness to shed light on Walker Davis's substance abuse and his complicated relationships with Paul Wright and his long-time girlfriend Brook Palmer." Brook stared straight ahead and didn't return my sympathetic glance. "Following Mr. Atwell will be Isabelle Brown, a classmate of Paul's and acquaintance of Walker Davis who will elaborate on the defendant's substance abuse.

"Lastly, we will call on Mitch McClung, the county medical examiner and forensic pathology to explain Paul's autopsy and prove his injury was not caused by an accidental fall, as the defense has alleged." Murmurs were heard around the room. Everyone knew this was the evidence likely to convince the jury of Walker's guilt.

"All of this," Batton continued, "will prove to you beyond a reasonable doubt that Walker Davis killed Paul Wright, committing murder in the second degree."

"Thank you, Mr. Batton," Judge Whitaker said, nodding. As Batton returned to his seat, Whitaker turned to the defense table. "And the opening statement from the defense?"

Mr. Johnson stood, checking his shirt to ensure it was still neatly tucked, and approached the bench. "Your Honor, ladies and gentlemen of the jury, the prosecution would like you to believe that this young man here," Johnson pointed to Walker, who looked calm and composed, "is not only capable of, but is guilty of committing a crime as wicked and terrible as murder. Today we will prove that Walker Davis is not guilty by calling three witnesses to the stand.

"First, we will call Clyde Jefferson to the stand to testify to Walker Davis's purity of character. We will then call Sheriff Ralph Jackson to prove that Walker Davis has no criminal record in this county. Our third and final witness to take the stand will be Great Smoky Mountains National Park Ranger Stephen Harlow, who will give annual statistics on injuries that occur on trails like Lonesome Valley Trail. Once our witnesses have testified, you will find it impossible to prove beyond a reasonable doubt Walker Davis committed murder. We will prove that he is most certainly not guilty."

Several minutes and procedural statements later, the first witness for the prosecution was on the stand.

"Place your left hand on the Bible and raise your right hand." The man obeyed. "Do you swear that the testimony you are about to give is the truth, the whole truth, and nothing but the truth?"

"I do."

Mr. Batton stood and walked toward the witness stand, a stack of papers in his right hand. "State your name and relation to this case," he ordered the witness.

"My name is Stephen Monroe. I live in Raleigh, but my family and I vacation to the mountains every spring."

"Is there anywhere in particular you like to visit when you are in town? Maybe somewhere you like to go hiking as a family?"

"Yes sir, we often hike in Lonesome Valley."

"I see," Batton continued, "and did you hike in Lonesome Valley on the morning of April 13 of this year?"

"Yes sir, we did."

I shifted uneasily on the hard wooden bench.

"Was there anyone else hiking in the valley that morning?"

"There were other cars at the trailhead, but we did not encounter anyone else on the trail."

"Do you remember the make and model of the other vehicles?"

"Yes sir, an old Toyota pickup truck and a red Chevrolet Camaro. In fact, I took a picture of the sunrise when we got to the trailhead and happened to capture the vehicles in the image."

I started to sweat and noticed Sheriff Jackson turn to look at me from across the aisle. We both knew my car was parked next to Walker's and Paul's. If the Bronco was in the photograph, I would immediately be pulled into the trial, something I was narrowly avoiding as is.

"What time was that?" Batton pressed.

"Around eight o'clock in the morning."

I breathed a sigh of relief. I had left just as the sun was rising, likely at seven. As it pertained to the case, I considered this to be weak evidence. Walk alleged that Paul fell while they were fishing together, so obviously their vehicles would both be there.

"The jury has been given a copy of the photographs that clearly show Walker Davis's truck parked alongside

Paul Wright's Camaro. This photograph was taken at eight in the morning on April 13. Walker has claimed that Paul fell from the waterfall on April 12, in the late afternoon, meaning Walker spent the night in the valley with a deceased or badly injured Paul. I find it disturbing that he did not immediately seek help." He let the silence linger for several moments. "That is all, Mr. Monroe, thank you for your testimony."

Mr. Johnson stood to begin his cross-examination. "Mr. Monroe. When you hiked in Lonesome Valley that morning, did you see either Paul Wright or Walker Davis?"

"No, sir."

"Did you see any sign of struggle or altercation?"

"No sir, I did not."

"In fact, did you notice anything, whatsoever, out of the ordinary that morning?"

"No."

"Okay, thank you. That is all." Mr. Johnson sat back down next to Walker.

The next witness to take the stand was Jake Atwell, the slimy self-described playboy Walker punched at the fall dance for making inappropriate moves on Maddy.

"What an arrogant prick," Brook said under her breath, while Jake was being sworn in.

Jake's combed, greased brown hair made him look more like an actor than a witness in a criminal trial.

He was loving his moment in the limelight. He smiled at some of his friends in the crowd as he took his seat, and I swear I saw him wink at Walker, whose jaw slightly clenched.

"Jake Atwell, you have claimed to be an acquaintance of Walker Davis, is that correct?" Batton started.

"Yes sir, I am." He smiled again.

"Do you attend the same school, or do you …" he trailed off, knowing good and well Walker wasn't in school.

"No sir, he's not in college. He dairy farms with his dad. We just let him hang out with my friend group."

Your friend group? Jake only had friends now because he was an "important" part of a murder trial.

"Objection," Johnson stated. "Relevance."

"Your social hierarchy is irrelevant to this case, young man," Judge Whitaker agreed.

"Apologies, Your Honor," Jake was quick to say. "I only mean to elaborate on how I know Mr. Davis." He added a sarcastic air to the formal title he gave Walker.

"Yes, please do, Mr. Atwell. Tell me this, how did you first meet Walker Davis?" Batton pressed.

"Walker first approached us when we started our first year at Brevard and offered to sell us marijuana. We declined, of course. Since then, he has been at many of our extracurricular events."

Several exaggerated gasps echoed through the courtroom at the mention of drugs. You would have thought Walker had sacrificed living animals to Baal. But in those days in the Bible Belt, smoking pot was considered profoundly sinful and symbolized rebellion against the laws of God and men, and therefore elicited a guttural response. Ironically, the people most vehemently against marijuana would likely have benefitted the most from its use. One of those such people was the older lady on the jury. She noticeably trembled.

Brook closed her eyes and shook her head. She had been badgering Walker about his reliance on marijuana for years.

"Do you mean to tell me that Walker Davis procures and distributes marijuana?" Batton continued, taking advantage of the horror of the crowd and jurors.

"I don't know if he does anymore, but that is certainly how I met him."

"Mr. Atwell—" Batton signaled to the crowd in the courtroom to lower their voices. "Have you ever had a physical altercation with Walker Davis?"

"Yes sir, I have."

"Can you tell the court what happened?"

"Sure. Last fall at our school dance, I respectfully approached Walker's girlfriend, Brook, and her friend to ask if either of them would dance with me."

"That lying bastard," I whispered to Brook.

"You know how emotionally unstable people become when they are on drugs—"

"Objection," Johnson called. "No foundation."

"Sustained." Judge Whitaker turned to Jake. "Mr. Atwell, you have no grounds to make inferences or assumptions. Mr. Batton is asking for details of your altercation, no more."

"Yes sir, sorry sir. Anyway, after I asked for the dance, Walker stormed across the dance floor and punched me square in the face, hard enough to almost knock me out." Jake shook his head in feigned sorrow. He was not the only person in the courtroom shaking his head. Two of the jurors looked distraught and were also shaking their heads, each mumbling something inaudible to themselves.

"Would you say in that moment Walker displayed jealousy over his relationship?"

"That's exactly what I'm saying. And honestly, I am quite sure the incident in April is reflective of that."

"Oh," Batton raised his eyebrows, "and why would you say that?"

"Well," Jake continued, "the week before Paul died, he told me he had gone on a date with Brook to Asheville."

"The same Brook who was dating Walker?"

"Yes sir, Brook Palmer. Although, at the time I don't believe they were dating anymore."

Brook buried her head in her hands. I could only barely see the edge of her right eye, which was squeezed tightly shut and trembling.

"That's not all." Jake looked at Walker as he said, "Paul and Brook kissed each other and maybe more, but he wouldn't say."

"Objection, Your Honor. Relevance."

"Overruled. It is relevant to the case," the judge responded.

The red-haired juror pressed her lips tightly together and nodded her head in apparent understanding.

"This is not going well," I said to Brook quietly, as I continued studying the jurors.

"I still can't shake this feeling that he might have done it," she whispered back in a desperate voice.

"Thank you very much, Mr. Atwell. That is all we needed to know." Batton looked satisfied with the testimony.

Moments later, Johnson was once again addressing the witness. "Mr. Atwell, have you had similar altercations like the one with Walker with other classmates?"

"I ... uh ..." He paused and looked around. "Well, yes, I suppose I have."

"Do you currently have a girlfriend?" Johnson continued, obviously confusing Jake.

"Objection," Batton called from the prosecutor's table. "Relevance. Mr. Atwell is not on trial."

"Goes to character, Your Honor," Johnson said.

"Overruled."

"No, sir." Jake finally responded meekly.

"Have you been forthcoming with romantic interests in other female classmates?"

"Your Honor!" Batton interrupted again.

"Get on with it, Mr. Johnson," Judge Whitaker warned.

"This is all to say that this is not your first time making advances on girls who may have been spoken for, is it, Mr. Atwell? This is after you have admitted to getting into physical altercations with other classmates. I am positing that these two things may be related."

"That is conclusory, Mr. Johnson and lacks foundation." Judge Whitaker passed his hand through the air as he spoke.

"Yes, Your Honor. No further questions." Mr. Johnson rested back in his chair.

One of the supposed farmers on the jury chuckled to himself. *He sees right through this bullshit*, I thought.

"Okay everybody, we are going to break for fifteen minutes, after which time we will reconvene for the final two witnesses from the prosecution." Judge Whitaker said as he checked the time on his wristwatch. Some people left the courtroom to stand in the sun for the intermission, but Brook and I remained planted in our seats.

"What hope is there, Chris?" Brook looked defeated. She had been watching the jurors as much as I had, and it was clear most of them were being convinced.

"I know, this is bad," I said. "But I do think at least one of the jurors was turned off by Jake's testimony. It was too bullish."

For the first time, I noticed Paul's family sitting in the front of the room on the right side, behind the prosecution. Paul's father was passionately talking to Mr. Batton, hands moving up and down, back and forth as he spoke. Paul's mother was quietly sitting next to him, clad in a black mourning gown. Her face looked more aged than when I'd seen her at the sheriff's office. She looked tired—no, exhausted. I felt guilty for not considering them throughout this whole process. I searched my soul for the reason. Initially, I was concerned for Walker. However, when I realized he was going to try to lie his way out of it, that feeling soured. As much as I loved him, it was out of my control. He was steering his own ship.

Why did I still feel the need to defend him? *Well*, I thought, *Brook*. Brook was the reason. Brook didn't kill anybody. Brook didn't lie about anything. Brook didn't ask for any of this to happen. She was as innocent as a little child. Further, it was likely my fault any of this happened to begin with. If I hadn't run to Brook on Christmas Eve, which caused her to immediately confront Walker, there is a chance they wouldn't have broken up, and none of these circumstances would ever have come to pass. It's likely that on the morning of April 12, I would have met Paul and Walker to fish, just like any other Friday. No breakup, no kiss, no fight, no death.

"The court is back in session, and I ask the prosecution to call their next witness." My thoughts were interrupted by a prompt Judge Whitaker.

Isabelle. Our classmate and Paul's date for the Fall Formal. Her testimony was nothing more than a character witness. When questioned by Batton, she went into great detail about Walker's drinking habits over the course of the spring. Of course, none of this was new information for the majority of those in attendance. Unfortunately, Walker had not hidden his dance with liquor after his breakup with Brook. He was often spotted downtown, slurring his words, cursing at judgmental passersby. Then there were the multiple occasions of vomiting and collapsing on the sidewalks downtown. Though it was known to many, the testimony did nothing to further endear Walker to the jury. The cross-examination from Johnson seemed more like a formality.

The final witness, however, was the most important for the prosecution. Once Isabelle returned to her classmates, Judge Whitaker addressed Mr. Batton. "It is my understanding you have one final witness to represent the state?"

"That's correct, sir. I would like to call to the stand the Transylvania medical examiner and forensic pathologist, Dr. Mitch McClung."

Mitch McClung wore dark-green slacks and a white, starched button down. He had an angular face with a pointed nose, on top of which rested bifocals. His receding black hairline was peppered with gray. His shoes were shined but somehow still dull, as if no amount of shine would revive shoes as old as their wearer. Again, there was a swearing-in before Dr. McClung took a seat on the witness stand. An ominous feeling of despair started weaseling its way out of my belly and into my throat.

"Dr. McClung, please explain your role in a criminal investigation for the court."

"I am a forensic pathologist and the county medical examiner," he responded with a thick southern twang.

"You are responsible for determining cause of death, if possible, correct?"

"That's correct."

"In the case of Paul Wright, were you able to determine cause of death?"

The room quieted, and all eyes fixated on the witness stand.

"Yes sir, I was."

"And what was your official determination?"

"Paul Wright died from blunt-force head trauma that resulted in fracturing of his cranium and associated damage and loss of blood to his brain." McClung spoke as if that much was obvious.

"What could have caused such an injury, in your professional opinion?" Batton questioned, glancing briefly at the jury.

"Well, clearly massive blunt-force trauma caused the injury. It is impossible to know what exactly caused that trauma, based solely on an autopsy."

"In the act of falling? Or perhaps by another person?"

"In my opinion, the absence of wounds on the remainder of Paul's body and the severity of the head trauma indicate he was struck by another person. Were it an injury from falling, one would expect to find multifocal lesions, meaning bruising or lacerations on other locations of the body."

A hum of voices briefly rose from around the room. Judge Whitaker quickly restored order and hushed the crowd. The jury seemed to be accepting every word of the prosecution and their witnesses. Walker and Mr. Johnson, for their part, were unchanged by the testimony and continued to sit with quiet dignity. Brook, on the other hand, buried her head in her hands.

The defense's best shot at swaying the jury was on Johnson's cross-examination of Dr. McClung.

"Dr. McClung," Johnson said firmly, "who physically performed the autopsy on Paul Wright's body?"

"I did, sir."

"Did anyone assist you with the procedure?"

"Several people were in the room," McClung said.

"That's not what I asked. Did anyone assist you with the autopsy?" Johnson pressed.

"Technically, I was the only one who interacted with the body, if that's what you're asking."

"Since the beginning of this process, it has come to our knowledge that you may not be impartial as a medical examiner."

"Objection, Your Honor!" Batton shouted from the prosecution table, over several audible gasps coming from the crowd.

"Overruled."

"In fact, Dr. McClung, it seems that you are well acquainted with the Wrights, Paul's parents. Would you consider that a true statement?"

"I graduated with them from the Medical University of South Carolina."

"Have you maintained a relationship with them since you all graduated?"

"Well, yes, we have kept up, but I assure you that did not influence Paul's autopsy whatsoever." McClung looked frustrated.

I nudged Brook's arm and nodded toward the jury. Several members made disapproving faces, and the elderly woman went so far as to roll her eyes.

This is what we need. Cast doubt, Johnson.

"In fact," McClung continued, "after this information was learned several weeks ago, the state sent pictures and notes from the autopsy to three other county medical examiners, who arrived at the same conclusion about Paul's cause of death."

I continued studying the jurors. The revelation about McClung's relationship with the Wrights seemed more impactful than McClung's explanation of second opinions. This is likely because in rural Appalachia, conflict of interest is an often encountered variable in the justice system. There are simply not enough people in tiny mountain towns. The mere suggestion that it played a part in the autopsy findings resonated with the mountain folk on the jury.

After several additional questions from Johnson, McClung left the stand, and we broke for lunch. Grady, Maddy, Brook, and I sat quietly in a red booth in the tin-walled barbecue restaurant, each of us deep in our own thoughts until Grady broke the silence.

"I think Johnson made up ground with the jury at the end there."

"The older lady and one of the bigger guys both reacted the way we hoped. We'll just have to see how the defense witnesses do this afternoon," I responded.

"I just can't shake this feeling that ..." Brook started, as she pushed beans back and forth in her paper bowl. "I don't know."

"What is it, Brook?" Maddy asked as she grabbed Brook's arm.

"I just don't know what I'm going to do if ... if ..." She started sobbing. "I don't know if I can live without Walker!"

Grady stared at his food, trying to hide tears that were forming in his eyes.

"Brook," I said, "look at me." She lifted her head and sorrowfully stared at me, causing chills to run down my chest and into my stomach. "This isn't going that badly. I think we have a really good shot. We have to stay strong."

A short time later, Mr. Johnson called Clyde to the stand, and we prepared to hear his character witness testimony.

"I lost my wife in 1978 to cancer," Clyde somberly stated from the stand, "and no one was more a friend—a comfort—to me than that young man right there." He pointed to Walk as his old eyes searched the room. "Everybody else, and I'm speaking to a lot of you men in here, come into my store all the time to buy flies and gear. None, not a one of you ever sits down and asks me how I'm doing. I believe in my heart that's the *only* reason that young man—" still pointing at Walker, "—ever came into my store. He asks me about my thoughts and feelings more than ... I mean, golly day, more than my damned wife did! The only trouble was when he was in high school, the principal would call up and tell me to send him back to class! Not politely, I may add." Pockets of hushed laughter made their way across the room. "I love that boy," Clyde said with a failing, crackly voice. He sniveled forcefully. "I mean, I really love him. I can't begin to imagine how any of you think he could do a thing like this." Wet eyes were dabbed all around me.

As I listened to Clyde's testimony, I thought of the impact Walker had on my life. He had taught me to have strong principles that were unbending and worth defending. He showed me that the best part of my life was always around the next bend of the river. Walker shared his spiritual connection with the mountains and the valleys and fostered such a burning love for nature in my heart that I'd never feel lost or alone in the forest again. We fought like hell at times over the years, but we always came out on the other side stronger and even thankful to have someone worth fighting with. Walk was more than a brother to me. Walker was a part of me, and I was a part of him.

It was hard to gauge how much the testimony resonated with the jury. The two likely farmers seemed the most emotionally invested, which made sense given Walker's upbringing. They shifted in their seats more than the other members, and one of them leaned in while Clyde spoke. I found myself wondering if Walker was innocent, even though I had been there the day he killed Paul. Batton himself seemed slightly moved by Clyde's words, if only because of the bravery and sorrow in the old man's voice. He forwent cross-examination.

Sheriff Jackson was called to the stand after Clyde. The defense questioned him on Walker's criminal record, or lack thereof, trying to reverse the picture painted by the previous character witnesses from the prosecution. Walker's record was unblemished, despite his rather renegade behavior, present since I first met him. The testimony was short and matter-of-fact. After several rounds of questions, Batton approached the bench.

"Regardless of Walker's criminal history, he was arrested by your office, correct?"

"Yes sir, that's right." The sheriff's face was red and sweaty, but no more so than usual. I tried to imagine how he was feeling, knowing my story and yet still testifying on Walker's behalf.

"And why was that?" Batton asked, in follow up. "Well, the circumstances of the case warranted further investigation."

"So, by your own department's standards, Walker Davis is a murder suspect, the only suspect in this case."

I think Batton meant it as a question, but it sounded more like a statement and thus elicited no response from the sheriff.

Realizing this, Batton asked, "Is that correct?"

"Oh," Jackson started, "yes sir, that is correct."

Batton elaborated on the aforementioned *circumstances* in further questioning of Sheriff Jackson prior to allowing him to leave the stand.

"Mr. Stephen Harlow, will you please take the stand?" Mr. Johnson asked.

A young man wearing a Smoky Mountains National Park uniform walked to the witness stand and was sworn in.

"Mr. Harlow, how long have you worked for the National Park Service?"

"Eleven years, sir," the ranger said in a surprisingly low voice.

"In that timeframe, have you acted as a first responder for injuries in the park?" Johnson asked.

"Absolutely. Multiple incidents every year, especially in the summer when the park is busy."

"What kind of injuries do you routinely treat?"

"The three most common calls we get are drowning, slipping and falling, and dangerous wildlife interactions. Drowning and falling are by far the most common."

"Objection, Your Honor. Relevance. Paul wasn't in the National Park," Batton called out.

"Overruled. Continue, Mr. Johnson."

"Thank you, Your Honor. The defense recognizes that the incident in question did not take place in the park, however, the environmental features of Lonesome Valley and the Smoky Mountains National Park are nearly identical. Mr. Harlow, do you have any statistics on number of accidental fatalities in the park system?"

"The annual average is just north of one hundred per year," the ranger said definitively.

Several heads nodded in the jury. *Good.*

"To summarize, would you say it is not uncommon to encounter people that have slipped and fallen to the point of being severely injured, when hiking or fishing in the Appalachian Mountains?"

"It is not uncommon. In fact, it's quite commonplace."

Batton was so eager to cross-examine Harlow's testimony, he could hardly wait until Johnson took his seat. I knew why, of course. The defense chose to use statistics to wow the jury, however, anyone with the capacity for critical thinking could easily counter the testimony.

"Mr. Harlow, have you ever responded to a call regarding an injury in Lonesome Valley?"

"No sir, I only operate in the park system," Harlow responded.

"Surely you have friends who have responded to injuries in Lonesome Valley?" Batton continued.

"I know several people who have helped lost parties on the Lonesome Valley trail system."

"Have they also responded to injuries?"

"Once, several years ago. A hiker had a dangerous encounter with a black bear."

I remembered the pain in my shoulder at the mention of the bear.

"But no traumatic injuries from falling?"

"No, sir."

"Mr. Harlow, the statistics you provided during questioning by the defense, are those specific to the Smoky Mountains National Park? Or are those reflective of the greater National Park system that encompasses all fifty states?"

"It's the entire park system," the ranger said.

"So, while that is a seemingly high number of annual fatalities, it does not directly reflect either the Smoky

Mountains National Park or, more importantly, Lonesome Valley. Thank you, Mr. Harlow. That is all."

It was a fair point, and I considered it a weak testimony. I looked at the jury as they started gathering themselves, preparing for the court to be dismissed. Shortly after, the judge addressed the jury and the crowd.

"All right, ladies and gentlemen, that concludes today's session. We will reconvene tomorrow morning at nine sharp for closing statements. When closing arguments are complete, the jury will deliberate for the time they need to produce a verdict," the judge announced, and just like that, day one of Walker's trial was over.

Chapter Twenty-Two

JULY 23, 1985

My stomach was in knots as I pulled into the parking lot at the county jail on the evening of July 23, after Walker's first day on trial. It was thirty minutes until sunset, and the shadows stretched across the cracked concrete sidewalk leading to the visitors' entrance. I grabbed the half-empty bottle of Jack Daniel's from the passenger-side floorboard and popped the cork. The slow liquid burn made its way into my belly after several discreet pours, and my nerves started to calm ... a little.

I glanced at my wristwatch. Fifteen minutes until eight—time to go see Walker. I ran my fingers through my hair, took a deep breath, and slowly stepped out of the Bronco. *It's just Walker. He asked you to come see him. You can do this.*

Ten minutes later, Walker joined me in the visitation room on the opposite side of a thick glass window.

I looked at the phone next to me and then down at my knee, which was bouncing up and down with anxiety. I used my left hand to still my knee and reached for the phone with my right.

"Walk," I said through the phone, nodding to my best friend.

"Howdy, Chris," he responded with a smile.

My eyes started burning, so I rubbed them with my shirt collar. "I miss you, Walker."

"I miss you too. It's nice to finally get to talk to you. Caught any big browns recently?" Of course, the first question out of Walker's mouth after months of being separated was about trout.

"I caught Big Unc," I responded.

Walker had been trying to catch the same massive brown trout in an offshoot of the Tuckasegee River for three years. The first time we saw it, both of us assumed it was a log on the bottom of the river. When it spooked, Walker jumped in the air in a mix of fear and ecstasy. We had spent dozens of hours the next couple of years going to the same spot, casting at the same fish, only to spook it time and time again. Walker named him "Big Uncle Brown" one of our last times fishing for him.

"Shut the hell up. Big Unc' is uncatchable, at least by you." He laughed.

"What if I told you Maddy caught him?"

Walker's face lost its air of humor, and he asked very seriously, "You're kidding, right?"

"Who knows, man. I guess you'll just have to think on it."

We stared at each other curiously for fifteen seconds or so, until the corner of my mouth started creeping upward. Walker tried to suppress his smile. I don't know who laughed first, but soon we were almost crying. Neither of us had laughed like that since Walker was arrested. The moment didn't seem that funny, but we both needed to laugh; it just bubbled over.

When we finally caught our breath, I asked him, "How are you doing, Walk?"

"I can't complain. This is vacation compared to working on that damned farm." His eyes widened as he remembered to say, "Thank you so much for helping Dad. He couldn't have done this without you."

"That's what friends are for," I reminded him.

"How are you?" he asked.

"I'm hanging in there. I'm worried about you—about the trial. I can't figure out what the jury is thinking."

"What are you thinking?" He studied my face.

"I—" I searched for words. I wasn't expecting to be put on the spot. "—I don't know. I could see them going either way at this point."

"That's not what I'm asking," he pressed. "I'm asking what do you think happened? Pretend you're on the jury. What would your decision be?"

I started feeling clammy. "I mean, you're innocent—not guilty, rather." I looked toward the phone and then the camera in the corner of the room.

Walker's gaze followed mine, and he said, "Apparently it doesn't work. One of the other guys said he overhead the guards say it doesn't record shit. But it doesn't matter, anyway. Are you sure you wouldn't say guilty?" His smile was gone, and he stared into my soul.

What is he doing?

"Yeah, man. I think—"

"Chris Avery, tell me right fucking now what your decision would be!" he loudly said through the phone.

"Guilty, Walker! I would say guilty."

To my surprise, Walker nodded proudly and sat back against his chair in victory. *My God, I have to tell him.*

"Walker, I have something to tell you. You can never tell anyone. You have to promise me you will never tell a soul what I am about to tell you. I should have told you a long time ago, but I couldn't make myself do it." My heart slammed against the back of my rib cage as I struggled to spit the words out.

"I know, Chris." Walker said quietly.

"I have to tell you—wait, what did you just say?" I froze in my seat and noticed the weight of every part of my body.

"I know."

"What do you know?" I asked, voice trembling.

"You're not as sneaky as you think you are, especially standing at the edge of a waterfall."

My head fell backward and rested against the cushion of the dirty, dark-green visitor's chair. "You never said anything," I whispered through the telephone.

"Neither did you."

"This whole time ... that morning in the parlor ... at the trial ... I was waiting for you to tell me. I wanted to help you, Walker!"

"I could say the same thing to you. I think it's better this way, though, since it's kept you out of the trial. Why do you think I didn't ask you to testify? When I heard you told the sheriff a made-up alibi, I just let it rest."

"Walker, I have been haunted by this for three months. I can barely sleep at night," I said, still reeling from his revelation.

"If it's any consolation, I'm not sleeping well either. How's Brook?" he asked, frowning.

"She's torn up, Walker. I won't lie to you. She is starting to suspect that you did it. She gets closer to that conclusion every day."

He closed his eyes.

"Walker, you've got to win this thing, if not for yourself then for her," I said.

"Chris, I don't think I can do this anymore. The only reason I've gone this far is for you, Brook, and my dad. It's tearing my soul apart." A tear trickled down his cheek. "I may be a lot of things, but I'm no liar. What happened was an accident, and I can live with the consequences. What I can't live with is a hollow conscience."

"What are you getting at?" I asked.

"I'm going to make this right ... tomorrow."

I thought instantly of Brook and how her heart would be fractured and about Grady knowing his son is a murderer. I thought of myself and how I'd lose my best friend for the rest of my life. I thought of Walker sitting in a cell, growing old in a cage. Years of memories flashed in my mind. I thought about first meeting Walker in the woods behind the farm as a child. I thought of our first trip to Lonesome Valley. The fall dance. The hayride. Sitting as a group on the old water tower. Then I thought of Paul.

"Okay," was the only word I produced.

Chapter Twenty-Three

JULY 24, 1985

"I THINK JOHNSON has cast enough doubt, but I guess we'll see," Grady said as we walked up the steps of the courthouse in the summer heat.

"Exactly, that's all he had to do. Beyond a reasonable doubt," I responded. Since leaving Walker the previous night, my mind could think of nothing other than our conversation, and talking with Grady about the trial over and over again was exhausting. *Will he really do it?* I wondered to myself.

Brook nodded gently but remained silent. I couldn't shake the feeling that Brook knew what happened that day. After all, she knew Walker better than the rest of us. I put my arm around her shoulders as we walked into the courtroom, ignoring the sweat that had soaked through her shirt.

We largely ignored the rest of the crowd and found seats about halfway down the left side of the aisle. The bench creaked under us as we sat down.

"Where's Maddy?" Grady asked me.

"She's on her way. I talked to her on the phone before leaving my house, and she was still getting ready." I looked toward the back of the room. "Here she comes now."

Maddy smiled at a couple of classmates as she made her way toward us. "How are y'all doing?" she asked as she squeezed past Grady at the end of the aisle to sit on my right.

"You know, the usual," Brook responded from the other side of me. They were the first words Brook had said that day.

"Hey now, everything is going to be okay, Brook Palmer." I picked her chin up to look at me. "No matter what happens, we are all going to be okay. I promise."

She didn't respond but turned her head away from me to stare back toward the front of the room, eyes glazed over. I said nothing else but reached to hold her hand. She squeezed back firmly.

I looked to the defense table, where Walker and Ben Johnson were having a heated discussion. Johnson looked frustrated, almost frantic. No one in the loud room seemed to notice, other than Grady. He extended his neck to peer over the crowd, eyes fixed on his son and his attorney. Johnson threw his hands up in the air while Walker continued talking to him, or rather, at him. Walker was calm but intensely passionate about whatever he was saying.

"What do you think that's about?" he asked when he noticed I was also watching.

You might be about to find out, I thought.

"I don't know. Maybe they are discussing their closing argument," I lied.

Several minutes later, Judge Whitaker called the court into session.

"It is trial day two for the criminal case North Carolina versus Walker Davis where the accused stands trial for murder in the second degree." He looked at Walker and his attorney and then turned to Horace Batton. "Today we will hear closing arguments, first from the prosecution and then from the defense." As the judge finished his sentence, I saw Mr. Johnson close his eyes and take a deep breath.

"Is the prosecution prepared to give its closing argument for the state?"

Before Batton could respond, Johnson rose and addressed the judge. "Your Honor."

"Yes, Mr. Johnson?"

It's happening. I looked at Brook and squeezed her hand again. I started feeling light-headed and nauseated. My hand started shaking, causing Brook to look at me. Her face turned pale when she saw my reaction to Mr. Johnson, and she quickly turned her attention back to the front of the room.

"The defense is not prepared to give a closing argument today." Several murmurs echoed through the courtroom. "The defense would like to ask for a change-of-plea hearing at the court's and Your Honor's earliest convenience. The defendant has decided to change the originally entered plea of 'not guilty' to 'guilty' for the charge of murder in the second degree."

The courtroom exploded into chaos, as all in attendance began talking and shouting at once. I heard one voice from somewhere over my left shoulder exclaim, "I knew it!"

"What is he doing?" Grady asked frantically as he leaned past Maddy to look at me. "Is he taking a plea bargain? Does he think he's going to lose?"

Brook still hadn't moved. It's as if she didn't hear what Johnson said.

I leaned toward Grady so he could hear me above the voices around us. I hadn't planned what I would tell him.

Fortunately for me, I didn't have to say anything because Brook, who had started crying, finally looked over at us and said between sobs, "Isn't it obvious, Grady?"

Grady looked confused initially. After a few seconds, though, his eyes narrowed, and he bowed his head.

"He did it. Walker killed Paul!" Brook rose to her feet and pushed past us toward the aisle, tears streaming down her innocent face. As she walked by me, she stopped and looked into my eyes. "You knew it, didn't you?"

I said nothing.

"I have to leave," she said as she tried to catch her breath. "I'm so sorry, Chris." Brook rounded the corner into the aisle and fled the courtroom, leaving behind the love of her life and her best friend.

I started to stand and chase her but remembered how little help I had been every other time I had tried to fix things recently. I had only made everything worse. I watched as she passed through the back door, buckled over in heartbreak. When I looked back to Grady, he was sitting forward with his head in his hands, Maddy gently rubbing his back.

A hearing was scheduled for Walker and Mr. Johnson to formally change his plea, and the court session ended with Walker's fate all but sealed. Maddy spent most of the evening at my house, as we sat on my bed, talking everything over. Everything would change now; Walker wasn't coming home. Where did that leave Davis Milk?

Where did it leave Brook? Where did it leave me, for that matter? I didn't have many friends. Walker and Brook were it for me. Most importantly, we talked about our futures, which we both agreed would be together.

After hours of reflection and mourning, very little was accomplished, and we decided to call it a night. I kissed Maddy good night as she walked to her car and slowly pulled down the gravel driveway, leaving me standing alone, surrounded by the sound of crickets in the forest. As I stood there watching her taillights, I decided I would never tell her I was there that day. She didn't need to know, and it wouldn't change anything at this point. It would be my sorrow to bear.

I tossed and turned in bed for what seemed like half the night. My mind wouldn't rest, and I couldn't think of anything besides Brook. It hurt me not to be with her that evening, affirming that she was going to be okay. I kept suppressing waves of anxiety that tried to overtake me. *I will go see her first thing in the morning*, I told myself, as I finally drifted to sleep sometime in the dead of night.

Chapter Twenty-Four

JULY 25, 1985

IN THE EARLY morning hours, I was pulled into a deep, vivid dream.

The trail stretched before me like a meandering path to the heavens, passing through thicket and holler, climbing and descending the ancient mounds of earth and stone. "Looking Glass Trail." Was it a thought or my voice? The words echoed around me in soft colors before mixing with the morning mist and disappearing through the canopy overhead. A strong gust of wind, full of whispers and emotions, pushed me from behind, beckoning me forward up the trail. The breeze seemed to breathe into me, making me feel light and graceful. I started to run.

I ran like the wind with all the creatures of the forest. Chipmunks and rabbits scurried between my strides. A doe bounded between hemlocks and pines to my right. Songbirds descended through the limbs of the trees and softly glided in front of me on the trail. I could almost reach them with extended fingers. A black bear sow and her cub walked somewhere on the trail ahead. All of them seemed to glisten with shifting light, and none of them left a mark on the forest. We all flew together with the updraft of the mountain toward an unknown end.

Colorful, speckled wisps seeped from the trees and flowers of the forest. I held out my hand, sifted a small amount coming from an unfurling fiddlehead fern, and brought my hand back to my face. With an open mouth, I inhaled deeply to smell and taste its sweetness. I appreciated the beauty of the forest as if it were my first and last time ever seeing it.

I looked down toward my feet but realized they were behind me. I was moving headlong up the path. Something else grabbed my attention; a sound permeated in the air around me. Though I knew there were no creeks at this point of Looking Glass Trail, the sound of flowing water filled my ears, my mind. What was first the delicate sound of a slow trickle was growing louder into the cacophony of a fully flowing river. When I looked again toward the trail, it became clear that the sound was coming from under me.

The dirt on the forest floor bubbled and welled like a creek, though instead of following gravity, it flowed upward, pulled along by some unknown force. I no longer traveled by my own will but rather floated along effortlessly, passing each tree, each boulder with enough time to watch them. A small sapling swayed in the breeze. As if time accelerated, the sapling began sprouting new branches that snaked upward. Each new limb was accompanied by a responsive thickening in the tree's trunk. Leaves emerged in waves, starting at the base of the limbs and extending to the slender tips. Light green turned rich and dark. When the leaves were at their largest, they started turning yellow, then orange, then brown. They fell quietly to the floor and flowed with me along the river—trail? Moments later, more branches, more leaves. When I took my eyes off the oak, I realized all the trees were behaving the same way. The forest seemed to breathe in water and life and breathe out leaves, over and over. It pulsated faster and faster as I was thrust higher. Surely, I'm close, I thought.

Fire. I was dumped from the flowing trail of the forest onto several acres of burning stone; I reached the top of Looking Glass Rock. Where the water from the trail poured onto the rock, steam lifted into the surrounding air. The forest was untouched by the eerie green flames. I walked slowly across the surface but was unscathed by the fire. I started hearing voices, though no one was around me. The voices grew louder in gusts of wind. Mr. Palmer's voice was the first I recognized. It dripped from the sky somewhere to my left and wrapped around my body before flying away. Maddy's voice approached from behind and gusted through *me, disarming me. I tried to see her in the breeze, but it was just a noise, a feeling. The voices were desperate, almost pleading, but I couldn't make out a single word.*

I continued forward toward the precipice, where the flat, hard surface sloped into a sheer rock face thousands of feet from the forest below. The next voice, oddly, was my own, though I did not speak it. It came from my right, seeping through the trees. A tingling feeling wrapped up my arms, as I could almost feel it pulling me backward. The last voice on the wind was Walker's. It did not come from behind me but rather seemed to be trapped in the updraft at the edge of the cliff. I followed it, one step at a time, until the slope became almost too steep to stand. I looked around at the mountains below. They beckoned me forward, inviting me to see them closer, more intimately. Walker's voice finally produced a tangible word, "Brook."

"That silly boy," I said, in a soft, feminine voice. With a final effort I reached out and jumped over the edge into the breeze, wrapped in all the voices of the whispering winds.

The feeling of falling violently pulled me from my dream, and I sat up as tears started building in my eyes. The brutal grip of sorrow wrenched my heart. "Noooo, Brook!" I cried in agony.

Chapter Twenty-Five

AUGUST 22, 1985

BROOK PALMER TOOK her own life on July 25, 1985, at around eight thirty in the morning, an hour after I woke from my dream. Two separate groups of hikers were resting at the top of Looking Glass and watched her abandon this world in search of a place that was happier, kinder.

By the time I reached the trailhead, police and first responders were already on the scene, turning people away from the parking lot. While I pleaded with them to let me through, a helicopter flew somewhere high overhead. I was too late. As I had realized the moment I opened my eyes that morning, my dream was more than just a nightmare; it was the manifestation of my deep soul bond with Brook. Somehow, I knew.

The world became colder that morning. I have spent the rest of my life trying to find the warm touch of Brook's spirit, but it's forever gone. My head hates her for abandoning us—me—but my heart continues to blamelessly love her. She couldn't handle the truth, that her soul mate was a murderer. Moreover, she probably held herself responsible for what happened to Paul after she kissed him. Regardless of how she felt about Walker, she would never see him again outside the walls of a prison.

I wake up at night still thinking of our last goodbye. The way she apologized before leaving the courtroom. The prolonged eye contact. Was it a call for help? Did she want me to stop her? I was so afraid of intervening after the previous few months that I may have missed the message hidden in her sorrowful brown eyes. Was she apologizing to me because she'd already decided to kill herself? Though I know it makes no difference now, I can't help but relive those moments. Heavy is the burden on my heart and my soul.

I didn't attend the next hearing or the sentencing. I locked myself in my room and mourned for weeks after Brook's suicide. Food lost its taste, and my appetite was stolen away by grief. I consumed little but water. With curtains drawn, I silently cried in the darkness. Initially, my mother called on me and tried to get me to open the door. I begged her to stop, at which point she resigned to leaving food by the door. I could not be comforted. My world was shattered.

When I finally emerged, with a broken heart delicately pieced together by sheer willpower and refusal to abandon my own life, I went to the only place I could find comfort. I spent weeks wandering through the old trails in the woods around my house and the Davises' farm. With every passing breeze, I hoped to hear Brook's voice call out to me. The heavy summer air laid ghastly mist upon the valleys. I thought if I extended my hand into the curtain of fog, I would find it taken up by hers.

Brook's ceremony was small and private. Maddy and I joined Mr. Palmer and a small crowd at a one-room Baptist church adjacent to one of the tributaries of the Davidson River. Her body was so broken from the fall, there was no open-casket viewing. It rained heavily that morning, and most of the eulogy was drowned out by the sound of water on the thin roof. I can't remember much else from that day. My memory of it was sequestered into the dark reaches of my mind as soon as I walked away.

The peaceful town was fractured. My classmates, who I had spent the four most formative years of my life with, disappeared overnight, moving on to other far and wide places, likely never to return to Brevard. Other than Maddy, I have seen none of them since Walker's trial. Mr. Palmer moved back to Charleston within a week of Brook killing herself. I never saw him again either.

I did, however, get to tell Grady goodbye. One morning in August my parents told me over breakfast they saw Grady loading up a trailer with household furniture and other items that indicated he was about to flee Brevard, following the flight of everyone else I knew. I gathered my stomach and walked through the cornfield toward their farmhouse, regretful that I had stopped helping Grady after the trial. At that point, though, it seemed futile, and I could make myself do little but sleep and eat, and even those were hard tasks. As I passed through the opening, I realized something was missing from their farm; the cows were all gone. *So, it's true. We have reached the end of Davis Milk.* I wiped a single tear from the corner of my left eye and continued walking. Grady was, with much frustrated effort, attempting to lift a large wooden trunk onto the front of the trailer that sat on the driveway between the barn and the house. Heavy sweat dripped from his forehead and drained out from underneath his ball cap.

"Let me help you," I said softly as I approached him from behind. He dropped the trunk to the ground and rested his hands on his knees, still facing away from me. I placed a gentle hand on his shoulder and turned him to face me.

"Chris," he said as our eyes met. He wiped his eyes with the sleeve of his dirt-caked shirt and then did the last thing I expected; Grady smiled. "Come here," he said as he embraced me in a loving hug. He patted me over and over, rubbing his hand firmly up and down the middle of my back.

I said the only words I could muster in the moment, "I'm sorry Grady. I—"

"You have nothing to be sorry for, Chris. I mean, damn it, you know as well as I do Walker did all this. You've been nothing but a friend to him."

"I guess he didn't make it easy on any of us, did he?" I said, trying to smile.

"Far from it."

"I just can't believe he's gone, Grady. I don't know what to do without him. I haven't felt so alone since the day I met Walker."

"But he's not gone. Walk is a good man, Chris. You and I both know that, deep down. But he deserves every bit of his sentence. He understands that. The important thing is that he's alive and has time to get right with God." He nodded when he said *God*. "And you aren't alone, Chris. You have your parents and that beautiful girlfriend of yours. Not to mention, you can go visit him when you're ready."

While I stood there listening to Grady speak, I prayed quietly he wouldn't bring up Brook. I didn't want to talk about it yet, and it would tarnish the moment we shared. He must have been thinking the same thing, for her name was never mentioned.

"So, what are you going to do now, Grady?" I asked as we lifted the trunk onto the trailer.

"There's nothing here for me now." After cranking the ratchet straps tight, he looked around at the property, the barns, the pastures. "This was all going to be Walker's, and I'm just getting too old to maintain it anymore. Dairy farming is a young man's game. I can't do it by myself. My brother lives in Knoxville and works in a steel mill. He told me he'd find a job for me and that I can live with him until I sell the farm and buy a house."

"A steel mill?" I exclaimed. "You can't be serious. If you're too old for farming, how are you going to survive working in a mill? And Knoxville? That nasty place?"

He shrugged. "What else am I to do? Besides, what are you going to do? From the looks of it, all your friends have moved away. Are you still going to Charleston?"

"I guess," I replied quietly, looking at the dirt below my feet. I kicked my heel into a soft spot of mud.

"Don't guess. You're too young to guess. You have too much to live for."

"I'll figure it out."

"You're damned right you will." He took on the same tone as my father from the past few months. "Well, Chris. I'd better get going." He held out his hand, and I took it.

"I'm gonna miss ya, Grady. Words can't describe how much you've meant to me. Thanks for everything."

"They can't describe how much you've meant to me either. All these years it's like I've had ..." He sniffled and dabbed his eyes again., "... it's like I've had two sons." He looked around at the property again and sighed. "I thought I'd never leave this place. Such a shame. Anyhow, if you're ever in Knoxville, come find me, ya hear?"

"You know I will. Bye, Grady." He tipped his hat and turned to check the hitch one last time.

A feeling of loneliness came over me as I walked back toward the trail to my house. Grady seemed to be the only remaining connection to Walk and Brook. My entire childhood was vanishing like a flash in a pan. My thoughts hung on Grady's words as my mind replayed them. *Dairy farming is a young man's game. I can't do it by myself. Besides, what are you going to do?* Grady's engine turned over, and the sound of gravel beneath tires filled the air behind me.

Whether it was God, destiny, or a rash, spur-of-the-moment decision, I'll never know, but a powerful conviction grasped my heart. I whipped back around and frantically sprinted toward the truck that was now halfway down the driveway. Grady didn't see me until I was even with the cab, at which point he slowed to a stop and manually rolled his passenger-side window down.

"Chris, what on Earth are you doing?"

"I can do it! I mean, we can do it!" I said between panting breaths.

"We can do what?"

"The dairy, Grady! Fuck Knoxville and fuck Charleston. You and me. We can run this place. I know enough to get by, and anything I don't know, you can teach me. I'm serious. This is the way it's supposed to be!"

I caught my breath while Grady stared at me, mouth agape. I continued, "My dad told me he had some money set aside for me to either invest or use to get my feet under me in Charleston. It's a decent amount ..."

"I'll be damned," Grady whispered.

"We both may be, but at least we'll be milking cows in hell together."

"Cows—damn it Chris, I already sold all the cows! Why'd you wait until now to make this offer, you old rascal?"

"To hell with those nasty old Johne's-ridden cows. We're getting new ones!"

Grady closed his eyes and started to laugh. It wasn't much more than a chuckle at first. Then I started laughing with him. After he parked his truck back by the house, we went inside and started talking numbers.

I guess I don't have to leave the mountains after all.

Chapter Twenty-Six

JUNE 18, 2018

HERE I SIT, all these years later, paces away from the very waterfall that changed our lives forever. As I look past the overgrown underbrush and rhododendron leaves, I can see the rock I knelt behind as I watched my best friend make the biggest mistake of his life. I look at the opposite bank, where my mind gave in to darkness and I fainted, almost into the water that surely would have drowned me. I think of Paul's image coming to me and pulling me from the water onto the cold sand where I slept through the night.

I wince at the memory of the large, black bear and my near mauling. I truly could have died multiple times that night. Through all the winding paths of terror, I somehow emerged on the other side alive. The same could not be said for Paul, or for Brook. I look past the letter in my hand at the cairns once more.

. . .

It had been early one morning in April when my phone started ringing. I ignored it at first and rolled over in bed, thinking whoever it was would leave a message. Again, it rang. Begrudgingly I got out of bed and walked to the dresser, where my phone vibrated incessantly. It was a call from the prison.

"Chris, it's Officer Jimmy Thompson. I have some bad news for you. Walker Davis passed this morning peacefully in his sleep."

"I understand," I responded somberly. Walker was diagnosed with pancreatic cancer three months previous and was being treated in the prison. The cancer wasn't responding to treatment, so we all began preparing for the inevitable.

"There is something else. Walker left a letter for you. He said not to give it to you until he passed."

"Yes, sir. I'll head down there after breakfast."

"Okay, I'll make sure it's waiting for you at the front desk." A long pause. "I'm sorry, Chris."

"It is what it is."

It's just like Walker to have written me a letter and not said anything about it before he died. He always had a flare for dramatic, hopeless romanticism. He lived his life like he was a fictional movie character. "That silly boy," I said out loud into the morning air, mimicking my long-lost friend.

It had taken me over a year to first visit Walker after he went to prison. I wasn't angry with him but seeing him would bring back every memory of Brook, freshening wounds that desperately needed to callus. Grady started visiting him much sooner than I had and assured me Walk wanted to see me.

It took several years for all the life to return to Walker's eyes, but largely my interactions with him over the last three decades were much the same as our relationship before the events of 1985, only without fly rods. We talked for hours, laughed together, and prayed together. I updated him monthly on my life at the dairy. It gave him pride and peace to know I was taking care of his father, and likewise Grady was taking care of me. It's the one part of Walker's life that persisted after he left us, and that helped to stave off depression.

Naturally, I showed him pictures of the trout I caught, with accompanying stories of the days spent on cool Appalachian waterways. His eyes always twinkled extra when listening to me vividly describe his favorite places with details about wildflowers, ancient trees, and colorful speckled brook trout.

I made him feel like a part of my love story, describing every date and every milestone. Walker may as well have been there next to me as I fell in love. He knew my thoughts, dreams, and fears as well as I knew them. He offered advice when needed and was a comfort when I faced the painstaking struggles of merging two lives, kind of like I once did for him a long, long time ago. As my best friend, Walker Davis was listed as my best man at my wedding. Though his place was empty beside me at the altar, everyone acted as though he was there for all of it.

Despite opening our lives to each other and broaching every possible subject, we never spoke of Brook or Paul. From the first visit to prison until my last, we pretended like none of it ever happened. If conversation started drifting toward the old days in ways that might involve Brook, one of us was always quick to change the subject. It was better that way. Neither one of us wanted to see the other one hurt, and talking about Brook Palmer would have opened the deepest wounds that either of us had ever known.

. . .

A cool updraft pulls me from my thoughts, and I see a large pink bloom fall from somewhere in the canopy into the creek and over the waterfall. *Okay*, I think to myself. *No more putting it off.*

Some of the ink words in the letter have smeared blots around them from being splashed with water from multiple fishing trips. They are still legible, however, and the style of the handwriting takes me back many years. I haven't seen Walker's handwriting since we were boys, and it somehow deepens the feeling in the pit of my stomach.

To my best friend, Chris,

Our childhood together passed like a morning rain in the spring. I wake every day with the desperate desire to go back and live it again. I long to crest another hill with you in search of a cascading waterfall, an untouched stand of hemlocks, or a quiet pine forest. The world was beautiful back then, at least the way I remember it. Adventure came calling with the rise of the sun and you came calling at the end of an early morning milking.

I try to imagine the cold taste of bottled whiskey on a winding, bumpy forest service road or the smell of barbecue drifting from downtown up the mountainside. I long for the days of chasing sunsets and sunrises. The days of believing we could summit any distant blue ridge or make it down any treacherous, swirling river. I miss the days of feeling alive.

As quickly as that time passed, these long thirty years have dragged on an eternity. I would have given into my loneliness and the creeping voices of the night if it weren't for you. You have saved my life every day since 1985 just by choosing to continue being a part of it. You have given me hope that the world is still beautiful outside of these walls. I have relished in your life as much as you have empathized with mine. Thank you for that.

I'm sorry for the hell I put you through. You deserved a better friend than I was to you. When you asked to help me, after everything happened with Paul, I should have let you. Despite knowing you saw it happen, I lied. I lied to you, I lied to Brook, I lied to my dad, and I lied to myself. I don't know why I did it, Chris. I have had years to question myself and the best I can come up with is that I was trying to protect Brook and my father from the truth. I was ashamed and didn't want it to ruin our lives. In trying to save everything, I actively succeeded in ruining mine and your lives, and I took Brook's life from her. I will never forgive myself for that.

The night you visited me, after the first day of the trial, I realized I had betrayed you and spiritually I shut down. I pitted your conscience against our friendship. I hope you can find somewhere deep in your heart to forgive me despite the fact I don't deserve it. I won't ask you to forgive me for Brook, because I can't even ask myself for that forgiveness. I have hated myself with a burning passion for what I did to her. Though the pain of cancer is sharp, it is nothing compared to the pain in my heart. I only hope that death is a relief.

I hope I can see her again, Chris. I have to believe I can make it right, since not in this life, maybe in the next. I hear her talk to me in the wind. I can also hear my mother. Here in the quiet of prison I have finally realized the mystery of the whispering winds. They are voices of loved ones that have moved on, whose spirits live in the freedom of the mountain air. Sometimes their voices break through, longing for me to be with them. It is almost my time, Chris. I am going to be with them soon. We will all be waiting for you up there—or out there somewhere in the wild. When you are ready, come be with us again and maybe it'll be like the old days. Until then, listen for me in the breeze.

I love you,
Walk

I read his words several times, sitting on my knees, before I finally put the letter down. I look at the cairns again before collapsing all the way forward, pressing my forehead into the soft forest floor. I dig my fingers into the rich soil and grab small handfuls as I close my hands into fists. "Of course, I forgive you, Walk," I whisper. "I forgave you a long time ago. You could have just asked."

The ever-climbing morning sun penetrates through the canopy to the forest floor around me, and the sound of rustling leaves starts to my left, and then my right. Suddenly, the entire forest begins to tremble in the gust of wind. The louder sound of rhododendron and oak leaves mixes with the soft hissing of pine needles. I listen with my ears and with my soul. For the briefest of seconds, I swear I can hear whispering. Though it's probably just my imagination, at the same time as the breeze, the mist hanging over the water at the top of the falls begins to lift and move upward into the clear sky, leaving me here in the clearing alone. When the wind finally dissipates, I stand up and brush my pants.

"Be free, Brook and Walk," I say. "I'll see you both soon enough." With the warm sun on my face, I begin the hike out of Lonesome Valley, my mind wondering what Maddy has made for lunch ahead of the afternoon milking.

Made in the USA
Middletown, DE
01 September 2024

60215342R00168